Sweet, Sweet Stories,
Some Sweeter than Others

Sweet, Sweet Stories, Some Sweeter than Others

by Daniel Curzon

Daniel Curzon

Sweet, Sweet Stories, Some Sweeter than Others

Published by l'Aleph – Sweden www.l-aleph.com

ISBN 978-91-7637-577-8

l'Aleph is a Wisehouse Imprint.

© Wisehouse 2017 – Sweden www.wisehouse-publishing.com

Contents

for ZACK

[Once upon a time, an old man with a flinty eye, arthritic hips, and an insistent double chin under his short, white beard decided that he had been too hard on other people, judging them harshly, unwilling to overlook their faults or forgive their failings. He had long thought he was balanced, both sympathizing with and condemning his fellow man. In his heart he knew that he was cynical and sneered at and excoriated far more than he wept for others. So he took up his pen and began to write sweet, sweet stories before he died. He wasn't sure if he could do a whole book of such tales before he sickened on the sweetness and threw up. Yet he vowed he would try. Below is the old guy's effort:]

SUFFER THE LITTLE CHILDREN

ROSS AND MAGGIE wanted to have a child, but they discovered that they could not. They had tried since they were married in their mid-twenties, to no avail. Now they were in their mid-thirties and a bit desperate. They were a nice couple and hadn't done anything to prevent them from conceiving: no drugs, no drinking, no Satanic rituals. Ross was too skinny, perhaps, but his sperm count was excellent. He was smart but had decided not to finish college. He had won the Best Bagger in the Southwest Prize two years running. He was good-natured, tipped lavishly even though poor, and looked after his elderly parents. Maggie was big-hearted and loved her sisters and friends with such enthusiasm sometimes people thought she was faking it. But she wasn't. She had grown up lonely despite having two sisters and wanted to make everybody happy. She was thin, too, and had to make her own dresses to get something not to hang on her.

They finally turned to Ross's father, who had sired twelve children with three wives. True, eight of the twelve had died young, but at least he seemed to know how to get a woman pregnant. Elijah T. Flint was eighty years old and looked like an Old Testament patriarch: wild, white hair that stood up in the slightest breeze, a white beard that he never trimmed, a rigid back, and a mean streak a mile wide. His idea of a joke was to leave a dead possum in your coffee pot. "It's the angle," the old man told his son. "You've got to mount your woman just so and deposit your semen upwards!" He made it sound like the Eleventh Commandment.

"We are thinking about adopting if we don't get pregnant soon," the son said.

"Don't say that!" the father chastised. "It's your woman that gets pregnant. Not you!"

"Pa, the man is part of it."

"Bunch of new-fangled hooey!" said the father.

"We love kids," Maggie, the daughter-in-law, was saying. "We'd also save somebody if we adopt."

They all sat around the rough-hewn dining table in Ross's parents' dilapidated old house. They looked like a Norman Rockwell painting, as seen through a fun house mirror.

"Doesn't the Bible forbid adoption?" the old patriarch snapped.

"I don't think so, Pa," the son said, although he wasn't sure.

"Well, it should!" his father said.

"Why are you so down on adopting?"

"Because people ought to take care of their own broods, that's why. Not palm them off onto other folks."

"But sometimes people, for one reason or another, can't cope or can't raise their children and need help."

His father was chewing tobacco and spat out a big wad on the floor in disgust. "It's a lot of irresponsible assholes refusing to take care of the offspring they bring into this world! If you can't take care of 'em, then don't have 'em – that's what I say. I had twelve of 'em and took care of every one!"

The son did not mention that eight of the twelve had died in infancy and it was his mother who had taken care of the twelve, first as char woman, then as third wife, from birth to death, without so much as a diaper change from his father. There she was right now, back in the kitchen, canning green beans. "Hi, you two!" she called from the kitchen.

"Come and visit!" Maggie called. She liked her husband's mother.

"I'm too busy!" Grandma called.

Despite the advice not to adopt, Ross and Maggie went to an Adoption Agency and put in an application. It was very complicated, with all sorts of rules and regulations. They wanted a child from Russia but were told that couldn't happen because Russia had stopped accepting applications from Americans, because of some international spat or other. So they said they would take a child from Romania.

"You're going to get a vampire!" Grandpa warned.

"I think they charge extra for that," his son said.

"Laugh all you like, but you mark my words! Genes! You have to have good genes!"

Meanwhile, Grandma had another baby, even though she was fifty-seven years old. She almost died this time, but she was sturdy stock and made it through.

Grandpa said to his son, "That's how you do it, boy!"

"Maybe we could adopt your baby?" Maggie asked, seeing how worn out and run down the new mother looked.

"Yeah, it would be in the family," Ross said.

"Oh, no, you don't!" said Grandpa. "Nobody's taking my child, not even my own flesh and blood." He did agree to build a new crib since the last one was so rickety.

Finally, after two years, the adopted child from Romania arrived at Maggie and Ross's home in Abilene. An agent from the Adoption Agency delivered the boy one dusty afternoon. Ross took time off from bagging at the Piggly Wiggly and Maggie took off some time at the Big Plains Beauty Salon to be home and welcoming when Bogdan arrived. They had seen a snapshot of him at the orphanage earlier, but it was out of focus and several years old. The real-life Bogdan turned out to look like a child movie star, now six years old and blond, the hair too blond, almost as if it were dyed. His eyes were large and a bit sunken, which gave him a heartbreaking, pitiful appearance. He spoke no English, but he didn't have to. He simply stood at the doorway and glowed.

Perhaps the story should end there. Alas, it didn't.

Bogdan started off fine, but then one of their cats died. It had last been seen with Bogdan.

It had been scalped. Bogdan, whose English had improved, said he knew nothing about the cat's untimely demise.

Then the boy started throwing himself against the walls in the house. He even fractured his nose and a shoulder blade, and the hospital staff investigated Ross and Maggie. They were cleared, but they were still under suspicion.

Bogdan attended the local school and did well, although he never spoke and didn't play with the other children.

"I just need to love him more!" Maggie cried.

"He'll grow up just fine," said Ross, who had been promoted to Head Bagger at the Piggly Wiggly.

"I told you so!" said Elijah T. Flint.

Maggie kept on loving the boy even after he poked her in the eye, and Ross kept on bragging on "my boy" even after he was caught shitting in their bedroom closet. "Can you send him back to Romania?" Grandpa asked sardonically.

Grandma had nothing to say, but she made sure her new baby was never alone with Bogdan.

Time went on, as it will, and Bogdan's blond hair turned brown and his eyes grew a little more sunken in their pits, and he looked less like a child movie star and more like an adult in a child's body.

"Give him time. Give him time," adoptive dad Ross said.

"I'll love him no matter what," said sweet Maggie.

Then both Grandma and her baby were found at the bottom of a cliff. The police said it was probably suicide, from the stress of having a child so late in life. Grandpa thought otherwise. "It's that adopted brat!" he wept. It was the first time in his life that Ross had seen his father cry.

Bogdan continued not to speak and to grow taller. He liked to hold his cold hands near the wood stove late at night when his "parents" were asleep.

Then Grandpa was found with his throat slit in the outhouse. He had died while wiping his butt with old newspapers. The police said it was unlikely a child could have done it – unless he had hidden there for days. Bogdan had been missing for several days but had no blood on his hands.

Ross and Maggie lasted until their mid-forties, when they were found dead from smoke inhalation. Luckily, Bogdan managed to escape, and was soon adopted by another desperate couple, who promised to "love him to death."

MORAL: Old Farts aren't always wrong.

[Are we sweet yet?]

TRUE STORY

I WAS TEACHING Air Force personnel in Asia in the early 1970s, when being gay in or near the U.S. military was considered a SIN, a SIN punishable by revulsion and expulsion. It was a primitive time in other ways, too. The copy machine was a rarefied invention, especially in Okinawa, where I was. A fax? What was that?! So if you wanted to get a copy of something that you had somehow managed to type up – and you were out of carbon paper – you had to go to inordinate ends to have such a treasure. I had to go to the Education Officer, a chubby sergeant with prominent bad teeth, well on his way to a career as a Lifer. I had to say I wanted any copies "for my classes." Other instructors lied in the same way, usually for their Christmas letters or resumes, or whatever. Nobody actually checked to make sure that they used the precious copies in their classes.

Except when they happened to be about THAT. THAT was anything gay. I was writing a novel called *The Y* (never published) and was trying to interest a literary agent in New York in taking it on.

I had no option but to go through the Education Officer.

He must have been very bored to bother to look at what I left in a folder on his desk. As I recall, it was hardly pornographic, or even overtly sexual, but it was HOMOSEXUAL. If the troops ever saw it, they would without question be fucking and sucking each other night and day and forgetting to kill the enemy. Who knew that HOMOSEXUALITY was so tempting to so many?! I thought it was "unnatural." That's what I'd been taught by Mother Church from birth, imprinting me with self-loathing and fear of sexual contact until I was twenty-six and a half years old. I had vowed to overcome my upbringing and bring light to the hostile world.

But the Education Officer had caught wind of my nefarious plot to HOMOSEXUALIZE the United States Military and turned me in to the Head of the University of Maryland Far East Division, a tall, ugly womanizer who liked to watch Thai female entertainers pop ping pong balls in and out of their vaginas. This man, Chancellor Kurt Luftwaffe, was equally appalled by my little gay lib chapter and told my immediate bosses, both deeply closeted gay men in their late forties, to fire me.

I remember meeting with the first boss somewhere in Tokyo. He was dying of leukemia at the time, although I didn't know that, nor did he, nor did it make him a nice person. He did not look particularly healthy, rather pallid, rather stocky. He was in a suit and tie despite the Tokyo heat and the poor ventilation in his office. I don't know what particular sex acts he was into, but I bet they were doozies. He asked me to resign. I said that I had just signed my contract for the upcoming year. He, Joe Stalin, or something like that, said they were not going to honor my contract because of what I had DONE.

"Oh, you're going to pay me for the year?" I said.

"Not likely," said he.

I was an early gay libber despite the dangers (especially shame) and was not going to lose my teaching job over this – as God was my witness! Of course, I was an atheist too, not exactly a help, all things considered. But I was a good-looking atheist, manly and humorous to boot. "I think the school's hands are tied," I joked.

"You cannot go back to Kadena Air Base," Stalin said – Dean Stalin. "You are banned from there, and so we cannot use you fully as a teacher."

"I'll teach at other bases, then," I said, though Kadena was my favorite.

"You don't seem to appreciate the seriousness of this," Dean Stalin informed me.

"Our textbook is full of articles about black issues, women's issues, minorities' issues. So why not gay issues?"

He looked at me as if I were crazy. "We will pay your way back," he said.

"What if I get a lawyer?" I said.

"Good luck with that!" he scoffed. "You're dealing with the U.S. Air Force!"

"Even Rome fell," I said.

"Because of homosexuality, wasn't it?" Dean Stalin opined.

"I think you'd better re-read your history, sir," I snapped. "I think it was lead poisoning of the ruling class, or maybe it was Roman military rations. Or American. The so-called 'decadence' of ancient Rome was actually Rome at its height."

"You presume to lecture me on this?"

"I am not actually defending 'decadence., I can take it or leave it!" I smiled, but it was too late for smiles. "The topic is so unspeakable, most people know absolutely nothing about it, except their fears."

And that was the end of my time with Dean Stalin. He sent me off to discuss my departure with the Under-Dean, Meredith Patsy. Under-Dean Meredith Patsy was a man, despite his name, and despite his fondness for rings. He had at least one on each finger of both hands, big and gaudy and probably expensive, like something Zsa Zsa Gabor would have worn in her heyday as a star. And yet nobody was trying to fire this Under-Dean for being GAY. Maybe it was his obviousness that made people think, Oh, somebody *that* flamboyant can't be what we think he is!

I had thought him a friend, because he had stayed with me in London when he was on vacation and because he had rehired me after I took some time off from grading PAPERS. But I was wrong.

He was a complete shit.

"Why in the world would you want to teach anything gay in your classes here?!" he said, looking over his glasses, which also seemed to be too glittery, or maybe I was just blinded by the situation I was in.

"Oh, I wasn't actually going to teach that chapter," I said. "I wanted to send it to a literary agent."

"Oh?"

"I appreciate the university giving me that publication award earlier this semester. I just hoped to add to my published works. I know the college looks good when its staff gets published."

"You think rather highly of yourself, it would seem," Patsy said.

"If I don't, who will?" I said playfully.

But Patsy wasn't playable. "You've admitted to mis-using the copy machine."

"What?" I panicked – I confess.

"Only items for classes can be duplicated." He was sure he had me pinned and wriggling.

"That's ludicrous. Other teachers 'mis-use' the copy machine. They – we – have no choice."

"I'm certain that if you read the rules you would be informed about what you can and can't bring to the copy machine."

"I checked in town outside the base. I could find nothing."

"So you abused the hand that feeds you," Patsy jabbed.

"I would hardly call it abuse. Perhaps I can reimburse the school for the cost of ink?"

"Don't be smart with me. Don't let the rings fool you!" Patsy showed downright evil teeth in that smile.

"I'm not being smart. I mean it. How much would the ink – and paper – cost?"

"It's a bit too late for that, don't you think?"

"You're not going to violate my trust, I hope – that I told you I wasn't actually going to use the material in my classes."

"I'm not?" Patsy said.

And sure enough, he blabbed my "confession" to Dean Stalin and to Chancellor Luftwaffe. Both of them drew up separate versions of my dismissal papers. I read them through several times and refused to sign them.

A hearing was thus called. I forget if it was literally called a "hearing." It may have euphemistically been labeled a "discussion," but a hearing it was.

It was held at the end of the term in a conference room with a long table at the University of Maryland Far East Division, Deans Stalin and Patsy on one side, along with faculty who agreed that I should be fired for my offense against the copy machine – to say nothing of the real issue: HOMOSEXUALITY.

I remember in particular one little pipsqueak in Poli Sci saying "This kind of disturbance of the norms cannot go unchallenged!" And lest I seem to suggest that everybody who was against me looked funny, there was also a very handsome Math instructor with salt and pepper pubic hair (sorry, I mean head hair) who was quite adamant that "Free speech does not apply in this instance, as perversion is not protected!"

There were, of course, some on the other side of the long table who stood up to defend me. One was a wonderful tennis player history teacher who was fucking some pilot's wife while the guy was off dropping bombs. Another was a young woman Science teacher who had a crush on me, God bless her.

It actually came down to a vote on whether I should be let go from my teaching position. It was close, but it shouldn't have been. The two deans voted against me, as did the absent chancellor, who had sent in his absentee ballot before the hearing. I won by one vote. There shouldn't have been a vote on it at all, for God's sake. Yes, the past is a foreign country. They do things differently there.

The vote at that hearing did not actually matter, legally. I was informed by a letter from the chancellor that I would no longer be able to teach at Kadena Air Base or at a Marine base nearby.

In fact, there would probably be no classes for me anywhere in their system and I would definitely not be offered a contract the next year. In other words, I could take my Gay Lib butt and get the hell out.

I was prepared to return for that final humiliating year at whatever pitiful base would have me.

BUT:

I had somehow applied for a one-year teaching position in Creative Writing at Fresno State University. I had put it out of my mind, thinking they would not, of course, want me at Fresno State. Wasn't Fresno a backwater? Wasn't it dry and homophobic there, too?

And yet, there I was being interviewed by eleven members of the English Department.

There was my GAY novel, the first gay protest novel, being passed around the table. But they were affable and friendly and asked me if I wanted to teach a Gay Studies class. Unbelievable! "If Fresno is ready, I'm certainly ready," I said.

Though there were two hundred twenty-five applicants for the one-year job, I was hired. I did not have to return to the unwelcoming embrace of the U.S. military after all. I came to California then and stayed there until I died – even after!

Eventually, even the awful U.S. military got rid of Don't Ask, Don't Tell and all other remnants of its anti-gay stupidity, and we all lived happily ever after. Didn't we? Of course we did!

Now for some Gay Reparations!

THE PRODUCER

PLAYWRIGHT VAN KIRKWOOD had quite the success with a twenty-minute play of his at the New York Showcase. The play was about a bisexual who tries to convince a person of indeterminate gender to join him in the Mile-High Club while on an airplane. The playwright had to withstand a "friend" of his (who was assistant director) calling it "a dirty play" and suffer through various cuts to the script and memory failure by the lead actor. The playwright likewise could not make it to NYC for any rehearsals or performances because he had developed blood clots in his lungs while vacationing in Merrie Olde England. Despite his persistent cough, run-down condition, and pale complexion, it had taken five different doctors' offices in Merrie Olde England to diagnose his condition. Ultimately, he'd had to fling himself on the ground in front of a National Health Service office in Stratford-upon-Avon to get treatment – literally. Despite the problems, the play itself went over very well. The audience, reportedly, was rooting for the bisexual to ride off into the sunset with the invisible fellow passenger of indeterminate gender, as the playwright had calculated they would. The playwright did not believe in phony happy endings, but he knew that theater audiences loved them.

The success of the little play led the playwright to some inter-actions with the Showcase's producer, Mr. Elon Scales. The interactions, by email and telephone, encouraged Mr. Kirkwood to expand his play into three scenes and hopefully into a likely Off-Broadway full-length play. Maybe even Broadway? Gregarious and rather pink, Producer Elon Scales was known to be a former hedge fund financier who had retired early from finance to go into major New York stage productions. One of them had starred a former Hollywood beauty now grown to four hundred pounds and had lasted for only twenty-eight performances on Broadway but evidently did great business on the road and thus turned a handsome profit. The playwright loved the husky voice and diva persona of the former Hollywood beauty, even at four hundred pounds, and asked the producer if he could possibly persuade her to take on the role of the bisexual's mother.

"I don't think we can afford her," he said. "But I suppose I could send her the script."

"Would you?" the playwright asked, playing it cool but thrilled to the core.

"Of course, there *are* some issues with the script," the producer said.

This was the first the playwright had heard of "issues" with his play. He had been told that the producer "loved" it. "Didn't we discuss having a backers' audition in New York?" he said.

"Oh, I'll need a Presentation Book for your script, to give to potential backers," the producer said.

Kirkwood wasn't exactly sure what a Presentation Book was, but he was pretty confident he could come up with one if it meant a backers' audition in New York City. "I'll do one," he offered.

"Just the usual – plot summary, potential audience, estimated costs, and so on."

"Done!" said the playwright. He knew how to read and wrote fast. So he was not afraid of the assignment. "Should we plan for the backers' audition before winter?" he asked.

"That might be good. There is one thing that troubled me during the Showcase."

"Oh? What was that?"

"I gave a note to your assistant director, a Mrs. Horowitz, I believe her name was. But apparently it never reached you."

"I guess not." It wasn't that silly request that the passenger of indeterminate gender be played by a living and breathing actor/actress, was it? Kirkwood thought.

"I thought the passenger on the airplane should *not* be invisible but should be played by somebody the audience could actually see."

"I see."

"We could believe in that character more that way. Don't you think?"

The playwright bit his tongue. No, he did not think the audience should see an actual person. No matter how good the acting might be, everyone would know within five seconds whether it was a man or a woman, and that would destroy the mystery, the theatricality of it all. "I guess I never got that note," he lied.

"Yes, I think we should aim for a real person to play the part," opined the producer.

Over my dead body, opined the playwright, to himself.

"I want you to have a very successful backers' presentation. I intend to invite some of my most reliable and trusted investors."

How am I going to keep my play's core with this man in charge?! The playwright rubbed his forehead, his eye sockets, and then his temples to prevent the headaches he could already feel coming.

"There is also the matter of the mother," Elon Scales said.

"And what matter is that?"

"The way she deals with the sadly disabled brother of the bisexual main character."

"Yes?"

"She spends a lot of time dealing with his attempted masturbation."

"But the disabled brother is *invisible*, so any audience would probably laugh about it."

"But having the disabled character play with himself?! Isn't it a bit … "

"It's funny! And that's also why the mother is fed up with care-giving and wants the bisexual brother to come back home to help out. There is no real problem without the sex. And it's not real sex. The invisible brother never actually does very much."

"Yes, I know. Still, it just seems to overstep a bit too much. Don't you think? And are the *disabled* ever funny, even if invisible?"

It's what makes the play edgy and contemporary! the playwright screamed into the phone, just not out loud.

He had taken the idea for a disabled brother with severe learning disabilities from a Facebook posting by his lead actor about his younger brother's fortieth birthday party. The family was trying to get him to smile, just once, but he wouldn't. He sat crumpled up and sour-faced as they sang "Happy Birthday" to him. That had inspired the playwright to escalate the family's problem into a masturbating, mentally challenged grown-up child that the mother was thoroughly tired of taking care of, without the writer having met anybody real at all. Such is the magic of Art!, Kirkwood thought. He likewise realized that he probably would no longer be able to use the same actor in the backers' audition because of the new material. It wasn't as though he had used actual people and actual events, but he supposed it was all too awkward to bring up the disabled and sex. And then the real brother went and died! Yes, better to go with a different actor, one who could, by the way, remember his lines as well.

"Couldn't you take out the sex parts?" the producer was saying. "I could look at them," Kirkwood said. He already knew that twenty of the twenty-five minutes of that scene were about the sexual misbehavior of the disabled brother. How was he going to change that?

They didn't communicate for several weeks. The terrible snows of NYC loomed ever closer.

"We could use puppets!" Kirkwood finally relented.

"What?"

"Puppets make everything funny."

"Are you sure? What kind of puppets?"

"The ones operated by sticks – so you can move the head, lift an arm. Maybe the passenger on the airplane in the earlier scene can be a puppet, too!"

"I do know some people who build puppets," the producer said. "Let me get back to you."

A week went by.

"They can build you one puppet for three thousand dollars and two for five thousand dollars."

"Yikes! That's a lot!"

"I think it's a bargain for New York."

Neither spoke of who was to pay for these puppets. Kirkwood assumed it would be him. He had noticed that millionaires tended to hang on to their money.

"They'll have to be puppets without genitals," the producer went on to say.

"Well, the disabled brother is male, not indeterminate," Kirkwood said.

"Have you thought about cutting the masturbation sections?" the producer pressed. "We have children in our audiences."

"We could ban children," Kirkwood joked.

"We do family fare in our Showcase."

"But the whole premise of the Mile-High Club in the first scene is quickie sex in the airplane's restroom."

The producer did not reply.

Was it possible he hadn't understood that? Wasn't he a New Yorker? Weren't they supposed to be sophisticated?

"It's one thing to flirt on an airplane and another to pull on oneself in front of an audience."

"But it's a puppet!" Kirkwood's throat was tightening up with the frustration of having to defend puppet sex. "Let me go through the script again," he finally said.

"Please do that. Couldn't you make the puppet of the disabled brother have a cold and therefore dab at his nose a lot?"

Oh, my God, did the man really believe an audience wanted to watch a distraught mother trying to stop her son from wiping his nose?

Time flew.

Kirkwood had assumed that the new scene would be part of the new season of the New York Showcase, so he got a young director to commit to the script. The young director even thought it was "wonderful." But the producer had not mentioned the backers' audition in some time and had asked Kirkwood if he had *entered* his play for the upcoming New York Showcase. I'd better submit it, just in case, he told himself. "Oh, I LOVED your airplane play!" one of the staff members told him.

Only this time, his new script was not picked. One minute they were discussing a backers' audition and the next he wasn't even in the Showcase.

Kirkwood read through his script again. It was clever; it was hilarious. It was out.

What had happened?

He frantically went through the script. Maybe he could make changes and still get it into the Showcase, where backers would see it and demand to put it on, starring the four-hundred-pound former Hollywood beauty! He could make the disabled brother not disabled after all, just unemployed, and the mother could be trying to help him get a job?! How lame! Or he could make the disabled brother into a refugee, and the mother is trying to make him stay although he wants to leave because he's too much of a burden?! Maybe he could make the disabled brother into a rescued, wounded raccoon, and the mother is afraid it might have rabies?! Maybe he could . . . oh, fuck!

Kirkwood did not make any of these silly changes. The Showcase went on without him.

He did not speak to the producer again, did not un-friend him on Facebook, and did not whine about the project that had fallen to pieces over disabled puppet sex.

Two years later, the producer put on a play about a four-hundred-pound former Hollywood star and her triumphant victory over her eating disorder. Kirkwood had been asked to write the script when the original playwright had died suddenly of a microbe he had caught in Sri Lanka on vacation.

It was a mammoth hit and quickly moved to Broadway and then into a miniseries on HBO, and everybody involved won multiple Emmys. Such is the magic of Art!

LOVERS, PARTNERS, FRIENDS

VAN NOTICED that his partner of thirty-six years, Shaun, had been sleeping a lot. He slept on the second couch in the front room, amid his litter, piles and piles of litter. They argued and sniped at each other like most long-term partners. They also hadn't had sex in years. When Shaun came into Van's bedroom and sat down on the bed to shoot up his insulin, Van decided to ask him about his health.

"You've been sleeping a lot," he remarked.

Shaun didn't speak much when he was smoking marijuana, which was most of the time, just when he had snorted some methamphetamine. "Yeah."

"Are you okay?"

"I guess so."

Van watched the needle going into Shaun's thigh. It made him feel queasy, but he was glad that Shaun was taking his insulin. His diabetes was bad, giving him neuropathy and low energy. His father and brother had died of the complications from diabetes before the age of sixty. Shaun was almost sixty-four. He still looked good, though, with a headful of dark hair and just a sprinkling of white hairs in the beard. And some dandruff. He had become a little bent over with time.

Van had osteoarthritis in his hips and was feeling poorly. He didn't like to talk about ill health, considering it too ordinary to discuss and also a sign of weakness. He kept himself reasonably together with Pradaxa, Metformin, Atorvastatin, Losartan, Flomax, and Vitamin D. He worried a bit about all the TV ads about "major bleeding events" from the Pradaxa. So far, though, he hadn't had any. He sat too much and watched men beat up each other in Mixed Martial Arts. Somehow that made him feel better. At least it passed the time. He was retired and bored out of his mind.

Shaun spread out the new beads he had purchased from a catalog. Lately he had taken to collecting beads, especially bright blue ones. He held one up for Van to inspect. "Isn't that beautiful?" he said. "Look at that blue!"

Van didn't care much for beads, but he said, "Beautiful!" with more enthusiasm than he really felt.

"You wouldn't know beauty if it ran you over," Shaun said. He put down the bead and picked up the silver dollar coin that had come in the mail that day. He also collected coins. "I wanted *uncirculated!*" he complained.

"Send it back."

"They make it hard to return them."

"It's a pretty coin." Van didn't care about coins, either.

"Thanks."

"Are we dying?" Van asked.

"Everybody's dying," Shaun said.

"Why are you sleeping so much?"

Shaun put the syringe back into its packaging. "Look at me! I'm taking my meds again." He popped a pill into his mouth.

"What's that?"

"Lyrica."

"Haven't you been taking your medicines until now?"

"No. Not for several weeks."

Van frowned. "Why not?"

"Because I wanted to die."

Van patted Shaun's pale thigh. "They're lovely, the coin, that blue bead. Lovely," he said.

They decided to have dinner out at a Thai restaurant and have pesto pot stickers, extra spicy.

HALF A SISTER

KIRKWOOD'S SISTER was named Doe Anne, or at least called that. Her real name was Joanne, but the name that Kirkwood had called her when he was a baby is what had stuck. She was nine years older than Kirkwood, had a different father, and was borderline retarded. He realized that "retarded" was no longer acceptable as a term, but he couldn't think of a better one. He'd seen terms go out of fashion and then come back in, so he didn't worry overmuch about it. His sister, over eighty, was good-natured most of the time, just don't ask her to do your taxes. She lived in another city in a small nursing home. Kirkwood had succeeded in getting her into one when her daughter, Lulu, had not. She'd been stubborn and preferred to be exploited by an illegal immigrant named Pedro, who stole Doe Anne's money when they went shopping at Safeway. Kirkwood did not think all illegal immigrants were bad. But Pedro certainly was.

"We're having a little problem with your sister," said the director of the nursing home on the telephone. He was a handsome, gray-haired man in his forties who ran the nursing home with his mother, who was sort of crazy.

"What seems to be the problem?" Kirkwood asked. He hoped that his sister hadn't died. He didn't want her to die, and he also didn't want to have to go to Phoenix to fix whatever the problem was. Phoenix was hot. Yeah, it was a dry heat, but it was so goddamned hot.

"I feel a bit uncomfortable bringing it up," said the director of the nursing home.

"Is my sister ill? She hasn't passed away, has she?"

"No, she's fine. She falls asleep playing cards sometimes and we had to get a new armchair in her room because of the soiling, but we decided not to charge you."

"Thanks. What is it, then?"

"Doe Anne keeps getting into the beds of our other residents."

"Does she get lost? I know she gets disoriented at times. That's why I insisted that she have her own private room. Is she …? "

"It's the male residents. She slips into their beds and waits for them to come to bed."

"Doe Anne does?"

"She's done it about fifteen times now."

"Is she scared? Is something scaring her?"

The director of the nursing home paused. "She says she wants some 'arm-lovin.'"

"Good grief."

He cleared his throat. "To be honest, she seems to want more than that. She takes off her nightgown and hides at the bottom of the bed. Then she pounces once the resident covers up. Doe Anne is small, as you know, and so they don't notice her at first."

"And there have been formal complaints?"

"Yes."

"I thought the heyday in the blood was over."

"What?"

"She's eighty-two."

"We've had two other residents threaten to move out unless she stops."

"It's sort of funny, isn't it?"

"We take that kind of thing very seriously here at Arid Hills."

"Really?"

"If a man did it, it would be called rape."

"So my eighty-two-year-old sister is raping men?"

"So far, no penetration has taken place, as best we can determine."

"She carries a dildo?"

"No, she is the one who wishes the penetration." He sounded very embarrassed.

"I don't know what to say."

"Do you think you could talk to your sister about it?"

"About being a rapist? I don't think so. She helped raise me."

"We may have to ask Doe Anne to move out."

"Oh, my God, it's that serious?"

"Maybe you could come to Phoenix … "

"And do what, buy a chastity belt? Chain her to her own bed?"

"Mr. Kirkwood, are you sure you're taking this as seriously as you should?"

"Horniness runs in our family."

There was silence on the other end of the line.

"Can you put Doe Anne on the line?" Kirkwood finally said.

It took a while to locate Doe Anne, and when she got to the telephone, she sounded breathy and crabby. "I was having me a nap!" she said. "What is it?"

Oh, my God, how did you handle such a problem? Yet Kirkwood prided himself on being forthright. "Doe Anne, you've got to stop hiding in the beds of the other residents there."

"Okay," she said.

And she did.

And that was that.

And then she died from a stroke while playing poker three months later.

She didn't wind up homeless on the streets of Phoenix or go to jail for rape, and that's probably more than you can expect from life.

A PECULIAR TALE OF A PECULIAR SICKNESS

MARIBELLE KRONE had been raised Roman Catholic in upstate New York, thinking that she had some vague Hungarian roots back there in the European darkness. It was a time in America when citizens tried to get away from their ethnic past instead of thrusting it into your face, like now. So Maribelle had never studied her genealogy in any way – a faded photograph in an old box at Nana's house, not nearly as interesting as Nana's kiffles cookies or Nana's almost-tame wild turkeys in the nearby meadow. Maribelle had always been a curious but fragile child with deeply black eyes and a sharp little chin; fragile but also mean in her own little-girl ways. She was known to chase cats up trees and camp down below and read for hours, making sure the cats couldn't get back down. She seemed to take particular delight when the fire department had to come and rescue the distressed animals. Maribelle soon took to drawing pictures of the cats crying pitifully. Today, parents of such a child would probably take her in for psychiatric examination, but this was half a century ago. Folks were not especially "sensitive" then, certainly not to animals.

Maribelle eventually grew up to be a well-known cartoonist of cats, who had her own exhibitions at the Metropolitan Museum in New York, the Sorbonne in Paris, and even at the Vatican, where one of the Popes developed Alzheimer's and became entranced with her "Tortured Kittens with Big Eyes" retrospective several years ago. She was often mentioned in the gossip columns of the popular press, even though she had a "serious art" reputation. Maribelle Krone was even once a category on "Jeopardy," although the contestants did not get a single one of "her" questions correct.

Rather famous and photographed more than most, she was not, however – how can I put this delicately? – not physically appealing.

She was six-two and spindly with long arms and bowed legs and tended to wear her hair in an old-fashioned, droopy style. She'd had but one date in college and asked the man to marry her. When he refused, she flew into a rage that lasted for months and then she accused the man of attempted rape. (Some of her finest and fiercest cat cartoons in *The New Yorker* came out of this period, according to most critics.)

When she reached the age of thirty-six, she felt sure that she was never going to find a husband. (I am pretty sure she even eyed me as a possibility but gave up when she discovered I was gay.) Then, lo and behold, she met a man on a panel on cat behavior: whether that can be altered or merely accepted. Arthwell Gibbon was deaf and stoned ninety-eight percent of the time and wore very thick eyeglasses because of his near-blindness; still, he found Maribelle fetching enough to soon ask for her hand in marriage. Alas, Arthwell tripped over a cat in Maribelle's apartment on the day they were to be wed and fell and impaled himself through the throat and bled to death while Maribelle was cartooning in the next room. (The gossip was that the relationship had not been consummated, both parties traditional Catholics and having waited for the ceremony to be performed before "partaking of" such carnal activities.)

So there Maribelle Krone was, still a virgin. Naturally, she had not even "touched herself," as they say in some circles. Truth be told, she did not have a very strong sex drive, her early thinness turning into outright anorexia in her thirties, draining her of any energy except for her cat cartoons, making her already flat breasts lie against her upper torso like . . . well, like deflated Whoopee cushions. She could not stand to look at herself naked in the mirror because she was so bony.

Her skin tone, on the other hand, was excellent, of a pallor much admired in previous ages.

By forty, she had begun to accept herself as an Old Maid, a thin figure of fun among the cartoon world's cognoscenti. She even began to give interviews in which she said she drank nothing but sugarless iced tea and ate but three small peas per meal, twice a day. She was said to model herself on one of the Saints Theresa. She found food disgusting, and the word "mastication" made her vomit whenever she heard it. She withdrew more and more from ordinary human interactions, while her house grew full of cats, as many as twenty-six at times, never fewer than fourteen. She did not really like cats, and many of them died in the unheated shed that she made them sleep in next to her brand-new house. She found their nearby howling, hissing, and fighting deeply comforting on those long winter nights in the Northeast, where she had moved.

Then one day at forty-three, she met the man who would change her life. It was not the most fortuitous meeting, since he had run over two of her cats by accident when he was visiting a neighbor of Maribelle's. But he had stopped his car and she had run into the street to see what had happened. There was an immediate spark. He did not know her to be a famous cat cartoonist, had never seen any of her work, so there was no question of his attempting to "cash in" on Maribelle's reputation in the art world. No, Harrison Overbreit was a scientist, fleshy-faced, ruddy, round-shouldered, aloof in demeanor, not a handsome man by any means, but he seemed unaware of the semi-Quasimodo cast to his presence or the limp that made his gait so charmingly eccentric, and so he carried himself with considerable confidence.

In no time, the two of them were engaged. Some questioned whether Maribelle had become involved with another man "rather too soon" following the unfortunate demise of her betrothed, Arthwell, but she dismissed the cavils as "beneath notice." Nevertheless, she did do a series of cat cartoons savaging her critics. When several fans sent her boxes of chocolates and candied fruits from an expensive retailer to show their support, Maribelle tossed them into the trash, unopened, and wrote a blistering op-ed piece in *The New York Times* about the "insensitivities of fans" for having made her, with her frail frame, have to carry such heavy gifts away to be disposed of. She did not care one tittle who she offended, for at last she had a man in her life, a man she was beginning to feel might love her, a man she herself could love. Could she offer him everything? No man had ever seen her "everything."

So that was the one fly in the ointment. She had let Harrison Overbreit kiss her on several occasions – and even on the lips, though, of course, for no more than seven seconds at a time (the time permitted by one of the encyclicals of Pius II). She had even let him rest his hand on her thigh in her garden, in front of the cats, no less. But they had not consummated the relationship in "that" way.

Even after they were formally married in St. Monica's Church in June, she had insisted on separate bedrooms in both their houses. Harrison said that he understood, said that he could and would be patient. His previous wife had frequently been sick and had resisted his advances on numerous occasions before she died – it was rumored.

Still, it had been six months now. Did Maribelle really expect him to wait much longer? For her part, she felt anxious and even guilty, knowing that she was expected to pay her "marital debt." However, her husband had never seen her without clothes on. Would he not be appalled by the concavity of her chest, the breasts little better than dugs now? She had no curves whatsoever, nothing to her hips, the arms muscleless. The face had even begun to have a certain sunken, cadaverous quality, particularly around the mouth. (Yes, yes, it is wrong to judge a woman by her looks, but looks have SOMETHING to do with getting married! Jesus! Get real.) Maribelle looked at a reflection of herself in a hunting knife, which she'd heard had once been used in the ritual slaughter of felines in some lost South American tribal society. "Oh, I am hideous to look at!" she cried out in true anguish. "I was never pretty, even though I prayed to God to be, and now I have starved myself into a pathetic ruin. I shall surely have to divorce Harrison. How can anyone expect him to make love to one such as I?!" She flung herself onto her bed in her separate bedroom and began to weep with the torrential tears of a maiden in an Old Tale. "Or I can kill myself!" she brightened. "I can stab myself in the eye and lie here until the cats devour my remains! It is only fitting that my life end this way!" Just then, the door to her bedroom opened. Maribelle's heart jumped into her mouth, and she began to shiver and shake. "Oh, no, I forgot to lock it!" she said aloud.

"We need to speak," said her husband, limping into the bedroom slowly. She could not help noticing that he was wearing no trousers.

"Harrison, you are not wearing any trousers!" she exclaimed, clasping her hands together over her bosom, such as it was. "I am afraid that I cannot allow you ..."

He cut her off. "You don't have to do a thing, my dearest darling," he said, advancing farther into the room. "Lie there and let me do everything."

"Surely not *everything*!" she said.

"It is time, my precious. It is time."

"But I ... I'm ... My ..."

"You are all I have ever wanted in a woman. Call it a fetish, if you must, but I know what I like." He pointed to his engorged penis, which was hardly pornographic but not bad – it was rumored.

"And dare I ask *what* that might be?" she demurred.

He limped to the bed and reached out with one firm hand and ripped her blouse from her body. "Ah!" Harrison cried out in ecstasy as he gazed at her chest. "You are as thin as my wildest fantasies have ever been!"

"Are you sure?" Maribelle protested weakly, as she looked away.

"I thought I would never find the true woman of my lustful dreams, a woman with that aura of Buchenwald that turns me on like nothing else in the entire world!" He pointed to his engorgement. "Oh, darling, darling, do you not see that we were made for each other by God?!"

And that night – and sometimes even in the afternoon – they were both fulfilled, however much the cats in the shed next door might hiss, howl, or screech at the godawful sex sounds they overheard.

A CHRISTMAS MISTAKE

(A version of this story was first published in the *San Francisco Chronicle*, December 2005.)

A FEW YEARS ago, this was, I was walking across the Golden Gate Bridge on Christmas Eve, carrying my daughter, who was five at the time. It wasn't that late, but already it was getting dark. And cold. I told Tina that we should go home because she was a bit sniffly and needed to rest. "But I've never been *on* the bridge!" she said, trying to look un-sick and bright-eyed. "If I don't do it now, when will I?" She knew that she had a problem with her spine that made it hard for her to walk and that she was going to die early. In fact, she died before she turned six.

But that night we were happy, looking all around at the shining lights of the several cities that we could see from the bridge. Tina was bundled up, as I was, all nice and toasty. Just our faces were cold. We even had warm muffins, chocolate ones, that we had bought at a store on Lombard Street near the Crookedest Street in the World. "Do you want your muffin now?" I asked Tina.

"I'll wait a few minutes," she said. "I want to make it last." She touched her pocket, where the muffin was.

I gave her a kiss on the forehead, and we walked along a bit more. Just as we were about to turn back and go home and get completely warm, Tina spotted a man up ahead, one of his legs placed over the railing of the bridge. He wasn't that large a man, nor was he dressed in red, but he did have a bushy, white beard. "Look! It's Santa Claus!" Tina cried out. He was probably homeless.

"I don't think so," I said.

"Yes, it is!" my daughter insisted. "Can we go see him? Huh? *Please*!"

I didn't know what to do. I felt sorry for the man, who looked like he might very well be getting ready to jump, apparently neither seeing nor hearing us, so concentrated was he on the dark water below.

I made a decision that I have never regretted. About how many things in life can one say that?

Now holding my daughter in my arms, I moved toward the homeless man, who finally heard us and turned his head. The look of abject desolation in his drunken eyes was so searing that I could not come any closer. He looked back down at the water far below and hitched his body in an attempt to get his other leg over the railing.

"What's Santa doing?" my daughter asked. "He looks so skinny. Is he sick?" She skedaddled free of my arms and stood next to me.

My tongue was unable to form any words, and I was about to turn us back toward the way we'd come, sure there was nothing I could do to save the homeless man if he was that far gone, and I certainly did not want my daughter to see him commit suicide right before her eyes.

Yet before I could move, Tina started running toward the man, calling out to him. "Look what I have for you, Santa!" She was holding out her chocolate muffin, her little hand sticky because the muffin had gotten partly crushed in her coat pocket.

The homeless man looked back at us, wavering, his eyes gleaming in the lights from the cities all around us. He shook his head no.

"But you've got to keep your strength up!" Tina said. "I don't have any cookies and milk right now. But you can have my muffin. My daddy says it'll make you fat." Again she held it out.

"Don't want it no more," the homeless man mumbled and looked back toward the water. His body was poised.

"But you've got to deliver all the toys tonight, don't you? To all the boys and girls everywhere, isn't that right?"

"No, little girl, I don't."

"Including *me*!" Tina said.

The man's eyes flickered, then met mine, and then he laughed. "Okay, I guess I do," he finally said.

He took Tina's muffin, and I helped him down from the railing. He went his way carrying the chocolate muffin. And I took my sweet, sweet daughter home for that final Christmas.

THE MANY, MANY CHARMS of LADY HAMMER

(This story was first published by *Chelsea Station* magazine,
October 2014.)

COME BACK into my life, I beseech you, Lady Hammer. It has been over a year now since we quarreled. Let's not go into whose "fault" it was. We had so many wonderful times together in the past, it seems a shame to forfeit all that over some minor misunderstanding. Was our friendship really as vulnerable as that? I thought it had a solid foundation, built up from innumerable hours together. We went through thick and thin, with as much "For Better" and "For Worse" as any marriage might have – even though we were never "romantically involved," as they say. It seems to me that people overvalue conventional romantic relationships – "Will this man marry this woman?" – to the point of overlooking, even demeaning, other male-female relationships. Such other relationships form a significant part of many people's lives. I think ours did in *our* lives, don't you think?

I want to remind you of our times together and perhaps heal this rift between us. Think of this as a scrapbook of fond memories. I believe it is not too late to rescue "us," Van Kirkwood and Lady Hammer. I don't expect you to reply, at least not right away. Indeed, I won't send you this "scrapbook" until I finish it. I don't know when that might be. Maybe I will never finish it. After all, I am old now. Lots of people I have known are dead. Who knows, I could join them. Perhaps you won't even read it and simply return it unopened. One must always proceed cautiously with you, as you no doubt appreciate, even relish. Are you still living at your vacation home in Palm Springs? I have the address. I could send it there, and you could read it beside the pool. I hope you have been able to get the place in shape, not that it was shabby before. I do agree with you that it needed a new pool and a cabana for changing outdoors instead of having to go inside the house. And that gazebo you showed me the plans for looked very enticing, with its own Zen garden on the side. I think you are correct; it would enhance the property's value greatly, should you decide to "flip" the place, as you have done before with other properties. I hope that Palm Springs is not quite so warm as it was when I was there. I must say those temperatures in the nineties at eleven in the morning were hard to deal with. But I loved the way you affixed that spray device to the garage so that water droplets fanned out and cooled the back garden. You always were good at enhancing your environment. I guess I'm just not used to temperatures that hot since San Francisco is so much cooler. If it gets to eighty here, people scream bloody murder.

I hope that lump in your breast was a false alarm, or something that you were able to get remedied since you caught it so early. I hate to say it, but you were always a tiny bit vain about your breasts. I'm sure you would hate to see them tampered with in any way. I recall how you said that Frank Sinatra loved your breasts and couldn't seem to get enough of them. I'm sorry that your two times with Frank Sinatra left such a bad taste in your mouth. I know that he took advantage of you as a young assistant in Rome on one of his movies – and you a newlywed, too! He was truly a despicable cad in demanding the *droit de seigneur* (as I believe it's called) on his movie set. You were so amusing whenever we dined out in a public restaurant and a Sinatra song came on the sound system and you demanded that he be shut off immediately! Those waiters were always amazed at your fury.

How did those cosmetic laser treatments turn out? You weren't too pleased with the first one, right? You said it felt like "a thousand pinpricks from tiny devil dicks" on your face. Did you ever go back? You were worried about those two tiny age spots near your earlobe. But they were barely noticeable. Honestly! Your makeup usually covered them up completely. I think about having some laser treatments myself. I have a brown spot right near my nose that needs to go. I also could lose a few pounds – like fifty! I always appreciated your bravery in trying those cosmetic procedures first. I was more squeamish. When you told me that you had jumped up from the laser clinic's chair and knocked the device out of the assistant's hand and "fled to safety," I thought I would die laughing and certainly never try such a thing myself. But my brown spot is growing more unsightly day by day, and I will have to act sooner or later.

And what about those polyps on your vocal cords? They were benign, correct? It's so fortunate that your new husband has medical coverage, and that you could get treatment through his policy. There is nothing wrong with my vocal cords, I'm happy to report. I still sing, just not at the Met, shall we say. My "career" as a baritone is still on hold. I'm grateful for the "gigs" I had here and there over the years, but a Household Name does not seem to be my destiny. I tried recording my voice on a new digital whatchamacallit the other day. It sounded a little gaspy, alas. I don't have as much energy for that kind of thing as I once did. I do have an idea for a new song, but we'll see.

Have you finished that translation of the screenplay from Italian to English? That was high on your priority list when last we spoke. I hope my notes on the translation were helpful. Don't take less than one hundred thousand dollars for it!

Oh, and how is your husband doing? Prostate problems are no laughing matter – except when they *are*, like when you pee on yourself when you hit a high note. (Guess who!) Tell Beau I said hello. I hope you two have ironed out your difficulties. It's never easy being in a marriage. Just ask my Janos, even though technically, we're not married. We could be "legal" now, but I think we passed that need, that phase some time ago. Janos asked me what I'm writing, and when I told him I was writing to Zooly, he said to say hello. He always liked you, and I think you liked Janos. (You didn't know the Janos that I know, of course, let me add snarkily!)

I'm looking at a photograph I took with my smartphone when we last visited. Remember, I asked the cleaning lady to take the picture of the two of us, with the water droplets showering us. You look like you could be forty-nine instead of seventy-four. You always had good teeth, and that new short "blonde" hair style suits you. And, no, I don't think the dark permanent eye liner clashes too much with the hair. (You did ask me what I thought, remember.) You look rested and regal, with your best Lady Hammer expression on your face: "I'm not sure what is happening here exactly, but I am in control of it, or soon will be!" I look sort of dorky. I've never taken a good picture in my life. I look every bit as old as my seventy-four years, and the dye on my mustache is pretty obvious and stains the skin on one side. I do think the "coloring" on my hair, now that I have finally done it, looks professional. My "colorist" (from Hong Kong) does a much better job than I ever could. So there we are in my "scrapbook," you looking as genuinely royal as you are, with that beautiful aristocratic nose, and me looking like an ambitious, pug-nosed peasant, but a peasant nonetheless. Ah, what a pair we made!

***

Do you recall how we met? It was in London, in that theatre course that you admitted later you had signed up for by mistake, thinking it was some other course. "The emphasis on musical theatre leaves me cold. I believe we're in a cult" were your first words to me, in response to my question about how you were enjoying the course. Music never seem to appeal to you all that much, it seems. You were content to turn off the radio in my car and drive in silence or with intermittent conversation rather than to have "ordinary music" surrounding us. Even when I bought that CD of madrigals, you were not impressed. "Oh, must we have sound for sound's sake!" you said on more than one occasion. You could be quite snippy in those early days. But I was determined to make you like me and didn't argue about the music.

I suppose I stalked you in a way during that first week of the theatre course. Did you realize that? When we sat around in our chairs in that big circle, the forty of us, in that first meeting and introduced ourselves, I must admit that I was very impressed when you said you were "just passing through" at that time, on your way to a series of spa treatments in Hungary with Princess Diana's favorite masseur. Princess Diana was still alive then. I thought, how exciting to be going for spa treatments anywhere, never mind Hungary. I also recall you later complaining, amusingly, about the awful hotel accommodations Dr. Tibor had provided in Hungary and how the spa treatments had consisted mostly of Dr. Tibor trying to massage his female clients below their waists. And when I heard you say that you were renting a place in Malibu "for a year or two," I confess I was smitten. Not sexually, just socially. My small-town Illinois self was thrilled with the possibility of associating with somebody with your glamour. Did you ever read Jane Austen's *Pride and Prejudice*? She has the heroine admit, tongue in cheek, that she began to love Mr. Darcy when first she laid her eyes on Pemberley, his wonderful estate. The fact that Elizabeth Bennet later comes to love the man himself is very similar to how I came to feel about you personally. It wasn't just the spas in Hungary and the rented beach house in Malibu. It was the whole package.

Lest you think I was merely a social climber at the time, let me remind you that you never mentioned your royal ancestry, not for a month at least. You had learned that Americans are not impressed by "royal lineage" the way the Brits might be. In fact, they are usually quite turned off by anything that smacks of "I am superior because my ancient relatives had titles or I have a title." Oh, sure, Americans gawk at a royal wedding or a royal scandal, but they don't really, deep in their hearts, believe that others are superior to them by birth. I didn't believe it either, though I certainly did lean toward respecting the Upper Class because it was brave and unself-conscious and demanding, all things I felt I lacked myself. You definitely seemed to confirm my expectations in those first days. I think you changed your flight back to California at least five times! And you convinced the airline not to charge you for even one alteration, let alone five. My thought at the time: How thrilling. I would let them charge me five times – if I even had the gumption to change the reservation at all. I would probably sit in an airport overnight and take whatever they decided to give me. But you, Lady Hammer, you didn't take crap from anybody!

**

Was it that first trip to London or the second, when I went looking for you in that rain? I seem to recall that you were in a pavilion of some kind inside a park. You called me out of the blue and asked me to join you for lunch. Was that the private club that your friend Estella Wentby belonged to? Or was that another time? They are sort of blended in my mind. I can still see Estella sitting there in the restaurant of this huge private park within London, looking totally miserable and even unhealthy. She was going through her divorce and also trying to get a nephew or somebody onto the membership list. She was livid and barely noticed me at all. As for the time in the rain, it may have been Hyde Park. You had gone to a knitting goods display or some such and you had suddenly thought, "Van is here! I must see if he can join me." I had just arrived and was jet-lagged and disoriented, but it was exciting to hear your voice on the phone, and I set off at once to find you. I took a bus and the Tube, maybe two of each, getting a bit lost, and when I finally found the park and was hurrying across the grass, it began to rain, as it will in England, and I got thoroughly drenched. I remember that the park seemed endless, but I kept half-running, half-walking to that pavilion, my hair plastered to my head, my shirt soaked. Even my pant legs were muddy. And then, just when I had given up all hope of finding you, you emerged from the pavilion a hundred yards away and waved a royal hand in my direction. "Van, is that you?!" you asked with genuine curiosity, as though the rain-soaked me was impenetrable. "I made it!" I gasped. And then you said, "Oh, I ate a bite because I thought you weren't coming. When I saw the rain, I thought, 'Van won't come out in this, and I had best take some nourishment.'"

You were so casual about it all, amazed that I had run through the rain, and yet you were likewise solicitous about whether I might catch a cold. You insisted that we get some hot tea immediately – but no tea bags. Of course, I did catch a cold, a terrible one, that turned into bronchitis, and I was in misery for the next ten days. The second day, you had to run off to see your son's South African girlfriend, if I have it right. She was in London for a day or so. You told me later that you wished you had stayed with me, because your son's girlfriend turned out to be "silly" and "selfish," and "a co-dependent," apparently meeting up with you only because your son had insisted, and eager to get away as soon as she could. You knitted me a sock during that period. It was supposed to be a pair, but somehow the second one never got finished. I still have it. It's too small and too ornate with that bright red band around the top, but I still cherish it. It's in an old suitcase I have in a linen closet, tucked away with lots of other memorabilia from our times together.

I wonder if you have saved anything from our times together. You were pretty ruthless, were you not, when it came to throwing things away? That expensive cashmere sweater that Anthony Quinn gave you, one of twelve in different colors, because of that unfortunate incident in Mykonos. That Gucci travel bag that you decided was an "atrocity" and tossed overboard without so much as a glance, on that ferry to the Isle of Man. And who can forget that husband you left buried in the sandy pebbles at Nice?! (I made up that last one – I *think*!) You always said that "one should not be saddled with any more baggage than a princess might need to escape the Huns." So perhaps you have no treasure trove of memorabilia after all. I was always telling you to write your memoirs, was I not? Perhaps I am ghostwriting them for you!

***

Do you recall when you "came out" as Lady Hammer? It was when some of the others in that theatre course in London wanted to go to the Ritz for tea. They kept calling it "high tea" instead of "afternoon tea," but you didn't say anything to clarify the Americans' misuse of the term. Secretly you may even have enjoyed it, almost patting them on their well-meaning but rather oafish heads in their desire to be seen in a fancy-schmancy hotel with their betters. Janelle from Florida decided that she would call to make the reservation for six. Naturally, the Ritz told her that it would be "impossible to book" for at least four months. Everybody was so disappointed. But then you stepped in and called. I was with you when you did. "This is Lady Hammer," you said in your most aristocratic tones. And before we could say "Blimey," you had secured the reservation for six the very next day. I could tell from their reaction on the phone, even though I couldn't see them, that the Ritz staff were bowing and scraping to accommodate this "Lady Hammer," as only the British and the class system can do. We all had such a good laugh about "fooling the Ritz," and then it came out, somehow, that you were not faking that accent at all. Americans almost never can do a credible British accent and can't seem to tell a cockney from an earl to save their souls. It dawned on me then that indeed, you must really be the genuine article, though the particulars about the Hammers being the right-hand men of several French kings from William the Conqueror on did not come forth for some time. I will give you credit for not boasting about your heritage. Still, you did use it to get advantages in England. Of course, the Americans in the theatre course embarrassed themselves all to hell at the actual afternoon tea by constantly jumping up and taking snapshots of each other, the "crumpets," the silver samovar, even the waiter holding the watercress sandwich tray. I can still see the maitre d' coming over to our table and saying, "Did Lady Hammer somehow hand you her reservation in the street?" Others also looked askance at our motley crew, who were so oblivious to how crudely they were coming across. You told the maitre d': "Oh, you must forgive them. They are Irish." Not one of us was Irish, actually, but it seemed to satisfy the maitre d'.

I always contrasted that meal at the Ritz with the ones I had with my brother, Willie, who is three years older than I am. His idea of an afternoon snack was "pig knuckles" on white bread, smeared with mayonnaise and devoured in about ten seconds, washed down with pink Kool-Aid, followed by multiple belches and farts, which he always found to be hilarious. Aren't you sorry that you never got to meet my brother? He is not doing too well at the moment, I've heard through the sporadic family grapevine. He now suffers from a choking syndrome of some sort, finds it hard to swallow. I suppose I could link it to his early eating habits, but more likely it's just genetic. We had different fathers, did I tell you? He took after his, with a slight frame and terrible acne with the scars that follow, and a sneer in every smile, again from some sort of lip deformity that he never had fixed. It's hard to imagine how two such different people as Willie and I managed to live in the same house for so many years. I have been thinking about my brother quite a bit lately. Not fondly. He was a jerk from the day I was born. Even last month he sent me a "birthday card" that asked if I was "still taking it up the ass." How does one reply to such a query? "Not so you'd notice"? "Every chance I get"? "Never did it even once"? "Shut your stupid mouth hole, you white nigger, or I will shovel your own mouth-shit back in with a trowel"? I'd trust you, Zooly, to come up with the "proper" response.

I'm a little bit worried about my partner. He has been staying out till all hours, coming home at eight or nine in the morning. Janos has always been a bit of a night owl, but at the age of sixty, he seems to be getting worse. It's not that we have ever been monogamous, just that we don't bring "tricks" home and fall in love with somebody else. Janos still looks very handsome at sixty, his head hair as dark chocolate as it ever was, just a few white strands in his beard, really quite attractive. He keeps his weight down by, alas, smoking far too much. He's on Chantix now to help him stop, but I am not hopeful. He calls me a nag about his "hoarding" problem. He calls it "collecting." What it is is the living room full of his old mail, much of it unopened, old magazines, catalogs, shirts, underwear (clean, thank God), and cardboard boxes and unused gadgets that he simply can't or won't throw away. He has also taken to lighting votive candles in front of the pictures of various "gurus" that he has stuck on the walls. I can't even go into the living room any longer lest I be buried under an avalanche of his stuff. I tried to "visit" with him the other night by sitting on the sofa that has a free space on it. Crap from the piles fell on my shoulders and legs. "This is a sickness!" I said. "You're right," Janos said. Of course, nothing has changed.

I'm also concerned that he may be eavesdropping, more likely Peep-Tom-ing, if that's a word, using my car to do it. I noticed a pair of binoculars in the compartment next to the driver's seat. They aren't mine. I guess I don't really want to know. Did I tell you about the arrest seven years ago? I may have kept it to myself. I was embarrassed. Janos was watching some guy dancing naked in his window (Hey, it's San Francisco!). With the marijuana and the speed, he thought the window dancer was having an affair with him. For all I know, maybe he was. In court, that guy denied doing anything in his window, but he did allow as how his *roommate* might have done it. Luckily, Janos got off with probation and a stay-away order. I just hope he's not once again spying through windows. So if he doesn't burn the place down with his votive candles, maybe he'll go to jail if he's caught again. He says I'm a "worrywart." It is what it is.

I'd like to believe that Janos wouldn't need to go out searching for his thrills if we had a better sex life. However, that is not true. He has always been out looking for "thrills" (more like "relief") in our thirty-three years together. I went out looking for a few of my own, just less so now. I don't want to burden you with too much detail about our private lives. I've always felt that you felt somewhat uncomfortable about my "gay lifestyle," although you disguised it. I'm sorry to say that I feel no sexual desire for Janos anymore. We had sex for twenty years. Maybe that's enough. It's probably more than most people get. The trouble is, Janos still wants to have sex. Just the other night, he said, "If I don't get some soon, I'm going to scream." Yesterday, he said, "We can still have sex. I don't mind." I didn't answer. Sometimes, he sits on the side of my bed and gives me that old look we used to use as a signal. But I keep typing away on my computer, seeming not to notice. It's not like I'm so attractive he can't keep his hands off me. There's just too much baggage – the hoarding, the binoculars, the fact that Janos never, ever comes, so many years together, a backlog of resentments. I suppose most couples continue to do "it" because they have no agreed-upon *other* outlet. At least with Janos and me, there are other outlets. I'll bet you there are more murders over sexual frustration than money! See, I am trying to count my blessings. I pay too many of his bills, as well. I think I am paying him NOT to have sex!

I remember when you asked me about fellatio, right after you married Beau. You said that you wanted to please him and he had requested some. You assumed I was some sort of expert on the practice. Perhaps you were correct. I think I told you to avoid employing teeth in any way. I suspect that was not easy, with your small mouth and what you implied was Beau's substantial size. You never said how it went, except that you didn't see much in it. I think gay men probably get more out of it than straight women do. Let's just say it's not a hardship. I was oddly flattered that you were open enough with me at the time to solicit my expertise.

By the way, did Beau ever express any jealousy about me and you? I realize that he knew I was gay and thus a remote threat for any hanky-panky. Yet it seems to me that straight men who have never had even one gay "experience" believe that any other man wants his woman in that way. The closest we ever came to such an "experience" was in Bucharest on that riverboat cruise, the stopover at that lovely hotel with the blue lights all around the bar. You had had one too many Cosmopolitans and I my two rum and Cokes, and, we were sitting opposite each other in those comfy, deep chairs, sharing past memories and being very intimate. I recall that look that came across your face, when it dawned on you that the moment was turning romantic, and you ordered a coffee from our waiter. I appreciated your good judgment then. I might have surrendered to the alcohol and the moment, and both of us would have been very sorry about it. In fact, it could have ended our friendship.

It's funny how little we know about other people's actual sex practices, despite the so-called Sexual Liberation of our time. You see the oddest people hooked up and I, at least, always wonder what they *do* in bed. Or next to the bed. Or in the pantry. In the bathtub? In the garage under the car?

By the way, how are you and Beau doing? I know that you filed the first papers for a divorce. Have you followed up? I know that this is a sensitive topic for you, but I continue to think that you should delay any divorce until you absolutely cannot delay any longer. You told me that your friend Estella Wentby says you're "mad" to leave Beau for such small offenses. I agree with her. Yes, he is trying to pull some financial high jinks on you with all those real estate purchases in Las Vegas and Long Beach, but would he really cheat his own wife? Have you gotten a second opinion from a real estate lawyer?

I confess I was a bit surprised when I got that fax from you in Las Vegas with the wedding picture. I had no idea how far along that relationship had developed. I know you made an ultimatum to Beau – no living together in his house without a marriage license – but suddenly, there you were, a married woman for the second time. I was very happy for you, knowing as I did that you were often lonely – despite my many letters! I recall you saying how sad you felt on Valentine's Day at the Marina, where you were living then, seeing all those couples when you had "nobody to kiss." And Beau in that wedding picture looked quite nice, very noble and solemn. He had managed to stand up from his wheelchair to hug you. Both of your eyes seemed a bit dazzled by the photographer's camera. Yet it seemed like a promising new start, despite his three earlier marriages. He didn't really seem to mind that you are nine years older than he is. He had "caught" you by looking at your driver's license.

What romantic relationship doesn't have some flaws in it, if we're honest? I am sure that you and Beau will work things out. I certainly hope so, and further hope that you don't act precipitously (as sometimes you do). There are times when I think about throwing Janos out – the condo is in my name alone. And throwing him to the wolves, somehow fitting with his family's background, the wilds of Slovenia in the Balkans. He has screwed up the sound system on my computer somehow, even though I have asked him to use his own – he says that his is "broken like my English." He also threw one of my CDs between the bookcase and a clothes tree yesterday. It was one of *my* CDs with me singing some of my own songs. He was supposedly "evaluating" the sound quality to see if I need to have it re-mastered. Somehow, Janos wound up critiquing my voice all to hell and then literally throwing the whole CD to drive home the point. (Yes, I am not speaking to him right now.)

Don't stop unburdening yourself about Beau or anything else you care to talk about. You hinted that you thought you might be "complaining" excessively, nagging your husband through me. I don't mind having my shoulder cried on. What are friends for if not that? It can't be all Eastern European river cruises, walks along the beach at Malibu, and drives in the Lake District! Remember that first trip we took together? I rented a car and we didn't include your name as a driver. You kept insisting what a good driver you were, and then we had that little unfortunate fender bender when you backed up at a light, in Grasmere, was it? The front bumper of that lady's car came right off. At least she was gracious about it. In the States, you'd have been shot! It was a bit dicey getting it all sorted out at the Hertz agency when we got back with all that damage still visible, even though you managed to spread some mud over part of it. We decided, as I recall, that it would be easier if I took the blame for the accident, rather than trying to explain why you were driving when your name wasn't on the agreement. We had some laughs over the whole thing. Of course, Hertz wouldn't rent to me the next year. Thank God for Avis. They try harder. (I like to think I try harder, too.)

***

A year and a half has passed since I wrote the section above. I have received emails from your daughter and even from you, mass emails that contain my email address. I don't know if they are meant to be a "feeler" from you or just an oversight about who remains in your email address book. I have not replied to yours.

***

Today, I got your letter, your snail-mail letter. I was somewhat shocked to hear from you. It's been three years. I was sorry to hear that Beau has died. I thought the treatments they have now for prostate cancer might have been more effective. I was sorry to hear that his children from his previous marriages are fighting you for a larger portion of the estate. I know you tried to strike up a relationship with Beau's children but they just weren't having it. I am sure you are correct – they were worried that you would supplant them in Beau's will. I am sure that you will prevail. You always seem to.

For some reason, an incident just popped into my head. Remember when we were in Palm Springs and Beau was sitting on the couch, visiting us for a weekend? Suddenly, he said, "I used to have nine inches. But I think I have lost some now."

What *does* one say to that? Do you want me to measure for you? I'm sure you have more than your share? As I recall, I said nothing. So did you.

Well, Beau has gone to his Reward now. I hope that you find a third husband.

I am glad that you will be coming to San Francisco next month, on business. It's nice to see you keeping active.

Unfortunately, I will be unable to see you when you are here. I am busily working on a new song cycle and simply can't take the time off. It may be my very last one, given my age. I have written plenty of songs over the years. If so few people have wanted to hear them, I can always comfort myself that I am "a niche artist." I certainly never wanted to be "pop," if that means what I know it to mean.

Our time apart has been difficult at times. I have not been able to find a friend that I can be as confessional and intimate with as you and I once were. My Janos is off most of his drugs now and I threw out some of his junk last week. There is so much of it, he didn't seem to notice! Good to hear from you.

***

Yes, I did get your telephone message when you were here. No, I wouldn't have been able to go out to dinner with you. I have been somewhat depressed of late. My cat has not come back for a week, and I fear the worst. He was rather feeble and even a bit demented. I made the decision years ago to let Buddy decide whether to go out or come in at his own choosing. I hate locking up pets. If he has died, at least he died free.

Janos has moved out. I can't say that I am sorry. He met a younger man who has a townhouse, and they seem to suit each other quite well. Janos and I had long since grown apart. Yes, I am lonely sometimes. I even expect to see him and his junk when I come through the front door. But he and it are gone. I sit in the living room now. It is very clean, even spacious. Maybe I will be too lonely eventually. Right now, I feel liberated.

I hope that you were not disappointed that I was not able to meet with you. I am sure we could have had lots of remembrances together.

This is our last communication. I do not mean to sound harsh, but I have undergone a sea-change. I have fallen out of love with England. The charms of the British Upper Classes seem to escape me now. Not that I have embraced the Lower Orders instead. They are as ignorant and coarse as they ever were. It's merely that I can find no one to root for anymore. I guess it is age. It is pre-death cutting off ties, abandoning the loves of the past. Letting it all go.

I had hoped when I began this little memoir that it would be a whole book and I would send it to you, you would read it, love it, and we would resume our friendship. We might have lost our closest loved ones, the both of us, but we might have had our special relationship to see us through our old age and final days.

However, I am not going to let that happen. I do not want to try to capture our "love" or whatever it was we had together. I'd rather that it be just a memory, fond or not-so-fond as it may be. Goodbye, my old friend, dearest Lady Hammer. We had what we had. And now we do not. I do think it best we remain with our fond memories instead of trying to recapture what we, no doubt, cannot. That would be even sadder.

O, YE OF LITTLE FAITH

KIRKWOOD HATED being in the hospital, especially under the circumstances. He had attempted to take advantage of the new medical technologies by having his own stem cells harvested from his upper butt and transferred to his hip joints to cure his osteoarthritis. Unfortunately, he had an infection in an upper tooth that couldn't wait to rush to his left hip as soon as the stem cells had been injected. He was thus unable to stand, could barely move his left leg, and wanted to die. In fact, he requested the End of Life documents from the staff of the health care facility where he was staying following the operation to clean out the septic infection in his hip. They refused to send them.

Most of the Filipino assistant nurses at Hebrew Meadows were attentive enough, though none of them were Hebrew. But Kirkwood tended to be "negative" and concentrated not on the ones who fed him and cleaned up his poop – from too much stool softener – and instead concentrated on how long it took them to answer the fucking call button and also on the nurses' assistant who had said to him, "So nobody's coming here to visit you?! What's wrong, Mister, you got no family?"

He *didn't* have a family, as a matter of fact, making her words sting even more. All his friends had died or disappeared via one quarrel or another. His partner of many years had not come to Hebrew Meadows even once and said that he didn't think he could make it because his own leg pains and depression wouldn't let up.

So Kirkwood sat in his room and watched CNN until he couldn't stand another minute of the "news" and tried to read a book about Patty Hearst on his Kindle, but that made him even more tired. He scooted from his bed into the wheelchair provided and rolled himself over to the window. There was a view of a freeway with cars whizzing back and forth, but that did not make him feel "free" at all, quite the opposite. He sat at the window and felt very sorry for himself.

"How is the view?" his roommate asked, pushing on his voice box button so that he could "talk." It was a metallic, android voice that gave Kirkwood the creeps, and he couldn't stand to look at it. The old man had had his larynx removed a year earlier, from the throat cancer. He also had some kind of second cancer in his brain. "I know I sound like a robot," he had said to Kirkwood when they'd first met, three days before. He seemed embarrassed by the device in his throat.

Kirkwood thought his roommate sounded like a robot, too. A bed-ridden robot. He didn't care if the old man talked to him or not. The man was a terrible roommate: tossing and turning, yelling at night. "Give me some saltine crackers and some little cartons of milk!" he would call out. "I'm in pain! Give me a Tylenol, for God's sake!"

"Jesus, give the man a Tylenol, for God's sake, so he'll shut up!" Kirkwood yelled, too. "When is my single room going to be available?!" he yelled some more.

"I need to get out of here!" he implored the evil-eyed, ugly, grumpy Filipino assistant nurse who never smiled and held her nose when she had to change Kirkwood's adult diaper. "Please, please, let me out into the hallway. Please!"

Finally, the assistant nurse grudgingly agreed and pushed Kirkwood out into the circular hallway, up against the second-floor railing that curved all the way around the floor. "Don't disturb me," she warned, "or I'll put you back in your room with Mr. Tylenol. I've got records to fill out." She pointed to her station – a small desk, her Station of the Cross.

"Oh, thank you, thank you!"

Kirkwood said, energetically but insincerely. "I won't bother you. I just can't stand hearing my roommate."

She was already gone, to her station. Kirkwood could still hear his roommate calling for saltine crackers and a Tylenol. At least his voice was fainter now.

Kirkwood looked over the railing, down at the first floor. He'd heard that there was a "zoo" down there somewhere – some finches and some rabbits, maybe a guinea pig or two. I want to see the "zoo," he told himself. I'd feel better if I made it to the "zoo."

He dozed, still slouched in the wheelchair, then heard some noises from down below. The nurses and nurses' assistants were wheeling in patients, it looked like. But these looked different. All sixteen were in wheelchairs, like he was, but they were bundled up like American Indian papooses, with only their faces showing. And every one of them looked ancient, dried up, asleep, half-asleep, and/or drugged. The staff was arranging the "papooses" in several rows and turning them so that they, all bundled up, faced in the same direction. Then the staff went off for coffee, or something. Light began to appear from the east and fall upon the old, old faces awaiting the sunrise.

The ugly, grumpy assistant nurse came over from her Station of the Cross and stared down at the sight. "They're Russian," she informed Kirkwood. "They're about to die. They have them face the sunrise." She shrugged.

Oh, my God! Kirkwood thought. It's a "zoo" all right. "Take me down there," he whispered to Ms. Grump.

"You stay here!" she scolded. "I put you back in your room with Mr. Saltine, you understand?!"

"Okay, okay," Kirkwood said. "You're not as bad off as them!" she spat at him as she returned to her paperwork. "They die soon!"

He held out as long as he could, until all the "papooses" were wheeled away, to their rooms, he guessed. Reluctantly, he wheeled himself back into his own room. His roommate was half-sprawled out, asleep on his bed on the other side, near the bathroom, saltine cracker wrappers on his stomach and chest. Kirkwood rolled himself closer to his roommate's bed, spying an unopened package of crackers.

He grabbed it from near the man's neck, noting the voice button. It was black, about the size of a halfdollar. Goddamn, I'd hate to have one of those in my throat, he thought. "Boo!" he said, without waking the roommate.

He set about unwrapping the package of crackers, but it wasn't easy. Not only were they "child-proof," they were "adult-proof." Eventually, Kirkwood got a finger through the cellophane or whatever the hell that was, and popped out a saltine. He bit into it and immediately regretted it. He reached for the carafe of water on the roommate's utility table but knocked it off and spilled all the remaining water. The saltine was not going to go down without a fight and stuck in Kirkwood's throat and would not budge. He tried pounding on his own back, to no avail. He couldn't reach far enough. He wiggled back and forth in his wheelchair, trying to dislodge the cracker in his throat. The roommate slept through it all.

Oh, God! I'm going to choke to death on a stolen saltine! Kirkwood swore at himself. Would it hurt for long? Would he black out? It was really hurting now. He felt his eyes begin to water, and he grasped the arms of the wheelchair.

All of a sudden, he heard a disembodied voice near him. He couldn't quite make out the words. Was it God telling him his time was up? Was it Satan welcoming him to his new home?

"Get this man some help!" the voice was saying now. It was coming from the ugly black button that amplified the actual sounds coming from his roommate's throat.

Kirkwood fell to the floor from the wheelchair, his eyes watering fiercely now. Just then, the ugly, grumpy assistant nurse rushed into the room. "Did I hear a call?" she asked, then began working her CPR on Kirkwood, sitting him up and giving him the Heimlich maneuver. The saltine cracker, in bits, flew out of his mouth. He began to breathe.

"I'm glad I could use my button to help you," Mr. Saltine said. It was the first time Kirkwood had seen the man smile. As much as he hated to admit it, the roommate with the ugly black button in his throat and the ugly, grumpy nurse's assistant had saved him from choking to death.

Did Kirkwood come back to the Church or convert to Judaism or marry Ms. Grumpy? Not on your life.

Did he send a box of saltine crackers and a bottle of Tylenol to the old man with the voice box for Hanukkah, before the man's cancers finally caught up with him that spring? He did.

HALF-BROTHER

IT WAS THE HOLIDAYS, so Kirkwood's family felt obliged to call and send cards. He never called them or sent them cards, so he was mystified as to why they kept contacting him. Cousin Leroy's musical Christmas cards arrived like clockwork. Aunt Sophie's always stale, broken brownies arrived, too.

Kirkwood was writing some new songs, a cycle based on his youthful experiences as the youngest child of his mother's second marriage and his mean half-brother, Willie. He had learned from his half-sister before she died that Willie had always resented Kirkwood. He did so because, when their mother married Kirkwood's father, there were two half-sisters already in the small house and so there was no room for the older Willie. He had been shipped off to his Uncle Othar and his wife. Willie was a bothersome, homely child, besides, always running off or playing with matches or scaring old small-town ladies with maniacal laughter at twilight. So sending him away was embraced by all, except Willie. He never forgot or forgave his mother. He especially hated Kirkwood, the baby who had taken his place.

Kirkwood had not known any of this most of his life. Back in the day, people didn't talk about their horrible family dysfunctions, let alone go on "The Jerry Springer Show" and indulge in them for an audience. He just knew that his half-brother didn't like him, was mean to him in ways that went unnoticed by their mother, and he took over a whole bedroom when he finally moved back "home" at twenty-three when Kirkwood was ten. Kirkwood could have shared the bedroom with Willie, but somehow he knew that would be even worse, and so he begged his mother to let him sleep on a daybed in her and his father's bedroom. He was a heavy sleeper and had no memory of his parents having sex. Or did he?!

So it was quite the coincidence that Willie himself called on New Year's Day and wanted to speak with his "baby brother." His voice was fragile and tired. "I have developed a condition," he explained." I can't swallow very well. Doe Anne, before she died, said that you tend to choke, too."

"Sometimes," Kirkwood admitted. He wondered if Willie still had those acne pits. Probably.

"So we have that in common. I'm calling from the hospital here in Hawthorne," Willie said. "I'd like you to come and visit me."

Kirkwood didn't reply.

"I guess I was pretty mean to you back then," Willie said.

"Were you?" Kirkwood pretended.

"My mommy sent me away cause of you."

"I'm sorry that happened to you." Kirkwood wasn't sorry at all. "You were . . . a handful, to say the least."

Willie laughed. "I sure was! Our mother had to put a dress on me and tie a rope around my waist out in the backyard." He laughed some more. "I made a very ugly girl."

"Maybe if you hadn't been so much trouble, she would have kept you."

"Naw, she had her cute little baby bundle!" Willie spat. "She didn't need or want me."

"You got to come back home eventually." Kirkwood was not going to litigate this.

"It took ten years and me in the Navy," Willie said. "But that's all behind us now." To Kirkwood, it sounded like Willie thought it had happened that very day. "Well, thanks for calling, Willie," Kirkwood said, trying to get off the phone.

"Are you coming down here to visit me before I die?"

The nakedness of the request had caught Kirkwood completely off guard.

"I'll try, Willie," Kirkwood said.

"That sounds like a lie."

"Okay, then let me say this: I don't think I'll be coming to Hawthorne any time soon."

"I think it's time we forgave each other, before I pass to the other side."

"Why should I forgive you, Willie? You were mean to me from the day I was brought home. I was never mean to you."

"You made my mommy kick me out of the house."

"No, I didn't. I was a baby!"

"She chose you over me. I was a troubled kid."

"Yeah, but you turned out all right. Didn't you?"

"I had a lovely woman named Irene who looked after me. Too bad you never met her. You would have liked her."

"I'm sure."

"She died last year."

"I'm sorry."

"She said you and I should make up. So did Doe Anne."

"Well, let's consider this telephone call just that. All is forgiven."

"You still sound mad."

"It was what it was. Life."

Willie hacked into the telephone, and it seemed that he was going to expire right then and there.

Eventually, he said, "Sorry. I can't control it. Do you ever choke this bad?"

"I've got to go, Willie," Kirkwood said.

"I heard some of them songs of yours."

"Oh?"

"Pretty."

"Thank you."

"And fancy. Is that what they call opera?"

"Song cycles."

"I don't know what they were about, but they was real pretty."

"You're too kind."

"I'm all alone now, with Irene gone. And Doe Anne gone, too. I never had no kids."

"My long-time partner is in the next room." Kirkwood knew he was bragging, but he couldn't stop himself. "He's a man," he added.

"Well, good for you," Willie said. "I'm glad you found yourself."

"Thank you." Willie was homophobic to his core. Still, it was nice to hear.

"So when can I expect you down here?" Willie said, too cheery.

"I'm not coming down there," Kirkwood said. "There's been too much bad blood under the bridge, or whatever the expression is."

"Oh?" Willie sounded surprised, a little hurt.

"I think it's too late."

"You do?"

"I'm not coming."

"I'm sorry I never asked you to come on my boat when I got one."

"That's okay. I get seasick easily."

"Well, I thought I'd try. Doe Anne said that I should at least try."

"I'm glad that you at least tried, Willie. I've got to go now."

"Maybe I could come up there, if I get out of this hospital."

"Don't overtax yourself."

"I guess you're really mad at me. I don't blame you. I was a shit."

"Goodbye, Willie. Have a good life."

"Bye, Van!" They both hung up at the same time.

Kirkwood did not go down to have a deathbed reconciliation with his estranged half-brother.

But after a few days he did find out which hospital he was in and sent a commercial card that said:

WHEN I COUNT MY BLESSINGS, I COUNT YOU TWICE.

He heard later from the hospital staff that Willie cried and cried and kissed the card about twenty times just before he passed away.

ELECTION

ONCE UPON A TIME, two opponents ran against each other to obtain the right to rule as Leader over their land. One of them was a Lesbian with a big bankroll and a bleeding heart that showed on her chest and who said all the kind things a liberal person was expected to say in that land. The other would-be Leader was a man with a constant erection, a Stepford wife, four slavishly devoted children, and an arsenal of dirty tricks and cruel put-downs on the tip of his tongue. They went at each other tooth and nail.

The Lesbian said that she would bring peace and justice and RIGHTS to one and all. The man, who was orange, said that he would drain the swamp that filled the land where they lived. The Orange Man promised he would bring back jobs in the tool-carving and buggy-whip industries and provide face cloths against the gases in the atmosphere. He vowed to keep the neighboring tribes out and to build a trench to keep them out, a trench with wooden spikes inside. He called the Lesbian "a big, fat Lesbian" and she called him "a horrible deplorable." Their campaigns went on for what seemed like years and years.

One day, all the citizens gathered in public squares around the land and voiced aloud their support or denunciation of the candidates for Leader. It got quite testy in some places. A black cat got caught on the wrong side of town and was crucified. An old woman was called a witch and doused with witch hazel and set afire. (Both the cat and the old woman survived and took up residence together.) When the votes were counted, by magistrates, it turned out that the kind-hearted Lesbian lost to the Orange Man by the slimmest of margins. Protesters took to the lanes and public squares to denounce the Orange Man. Anarchists emerged from the woodwork, as they will, and trashed various butcher shops and butteries. "It is the end of the world!" wept the losing side.

But it must be said that there was something in the outrageous victory of the Nasty Orange Man that did *not displease* most folk. Ahem . . .

And then one day, the Orange Man woke up and decided that he would become a Philosopher-King. From that day forward, he proclaimed nothing but wisdom, and all the people in that land lived prosperous and happy lives. And very dull ones. So they soon threw him out of office, because they craved excitement more than wisdom.

TRANSPLANT

LONG AGO, a man was having trouble walking. His right knee kept giving out. Three times he fell down on the bad road outside his hovel. The man was generally healthy, tall and strong and independent. Oh, and he was an agnostic. He lived alone except for a pet gopher that he had rescued from a sadistic neighbor who was going to sacrifice the gopher in some awful ritual. The man didn't actually like the gopher, nor did the gopher like the man. They pretty much stayed in different parts of the hovel.

When the man fell a fourth time, he went to see a doctor. The doctor was blind, hard of hearing, senile, and badly educated, but he came to a conclusion quickly. "You need a knee transplant," he told his patient.

"But won't that hurt?" gasped the patient.

"Exceedingly. Knee replacements won't be commonplace for hundreds of years."

"Are you certain we should try it now?"

"Do you want to keep falling down?"

"Not especially."

"Then come in next Tuesday and I will replace your knee with a device I have invented." The doctor pointed to a contraption on display on the rear wall. "It may have a few kinks that need to be worked out, but I guarantee you will be walking like a baby by next Thursday."

"You mean taking little steps and falling on my face?" the not-quite-convinced patient said. He glared at the contraption, which had all sorts of wires and straps and gewgaws on it.

"You will walk like a man of seventy!" the doctor promised.

"But I'm only forty-nine."

"Don't look a gift knee in the mouth," the doctor snapped. "Don't forget. I can always give it to someone else."

"How much will you charge?" the patient inquired.

"For you, it's free. All I want is your gopher."

"My gopher? What for?"

"I need a pet," the doctor said.

The patient didn't like the tenor of the conversation, but it was a way to get rid of the gopher.

"All right," he said.

"Bring the gopher with you next Tuesday." The doctor smiled and nodded at the false knee that was hanging on the wall.

At home, the gopher seemed to sense that the man with the bad knee was up to something and tried to cozy up to the owner of the hovel. He even got on the man's lap and showed his belly.

"Too late," the owner of the hovel said, putting the gopher on the dirt floor. The next Tuesday, he managed to carry the gopher to the doctor's office in a basket without getting scratched or bitten. The doctor peeked at the gopher and was pleased. "He'll do just fine," he said.

The patient was suspicious of the doctor's intent, but he knew that he required a new knee. "He's a good gopher," he said lamely. In his heart of hearts, he did not care anymore what might happen to the gopher.

"Come and lie on my operating table," said the doctor, leading the patient to a wooden board on two sawhorses. He removed the knee contraption from the wall.

"You're going to use *that* exact one?" the patient panicked.

"I didn't have time to make one just for you," the doctor said. "And beggars can't be choosy."

"Maybe we should … "

"Oh, shut up and get on the board!"

The patient climbed onto the board. It was not comfortable. "Don't you have any anesthetic?"

"What's that?" the doctor said.

"For my knee."

"Oh, it's your *knee* that's the problem?" the doctor said.

"You forgot it's my knee that's the problem?!" the patient said.

"I'm not the doctor I used to be."

"Jesus, Mary, and Joseph!" exclaimed the patient who lived in a hovel and had surrendered a gopher to get some relief for his knee pain.

"It shouldn't take more than an hour," the doctor said.

"That long?"

"What if I knock you out with this?" The doctor picked up a wooden mallet and tapped it against his palm.

"I suppose it's better than nothing."

"In the future, people won't feel a thing with operations like this." With that, the doctor raised the wooden mallet and banged the patient on the temple. The man went out as if hit by a wooden mallet.

When he came to, he looked down at his knee to see if he had a new one. So far as he could tell, there was no change. Was it possible the new knee was undetectable? He looked at the doctor, who was washing his bloodied hands in a basin.

"That was a tough one and my first!" the doctor said. "How you doing?"

The patient moved a little and felt a soreness in his butt. "Ouch!" he cried out.

"Yeah, you're probably going to be a little sore there for a while. Don't get the wound infected."

"Why is my knee untouched but my butt sore?" the patient asked.

"Well, I gave you what you wanted."

"You did?"

"I tore you a new one."

"You tore me a new what?"

"An asshole. That's what you asked for."

"No, I didn't!"

"Well, I thought you needed one. Your gopher, by the way, was delicious."

The patient eased himself off the operating board and ran screaming from the doctor's office, the pain in his butt making him hobble to his hovel.

The pain there went away, but the pain in his knee did not. So, much against his will, and since there was no other doctor around for miles, he went back to the same doctor and had a second operation. This time when he woke up, he noticed that his knee was still the same, yet his chest had obviously been cut open and then sewed shut. He looked at the doctor, who was at the basin cleaning up. "Doctor, did you forget my knee again?!" he cried out.

The doctor turned to him. "But I thought you wanted a new heart."

"No, I didn't."

"Well, that's what you got. How's it feel?"

The patient tapped the sutures on his chest. "Not bad, actually."

"Good. I got it from a nun who died at ninety."

"I feel blessed," the patient said.

"You should. I had to bribe the head nun to get the body."

"I feel like praying now." And the agnostic with the nun's heart began praying every day, and even founded a home for poor, mistreated gophers. Amen.

[Absolutely True Story!]

A HOUSE DIVIDED

YOU BASTARDS! Do you know what you've done? Admit it, you racist pricks! We were just out walking with our baby in a stroller. She was asleep and not bothering nobody, with that crinkly nose and beautiful chocolate face peeking out of the blanket. My girlfriend and future fiancée, Laquesha, was telling me how much she loved me and our baby and how she was gonna enroll in college and maybe beauty school, too. I was about to have a job interview the next day, to drive for Uber. I'm a good driver.

It was a beautiful, sunny day in the 'hood.

And then you had to go and spoil everything, just because I was wearing a black hoodie. Didn't your momma ever teach you not to judge a book by its cover? Yeah, I had a gun in my belt under my jacket, but you got to – to protect yourself where I live. Laquesha and me were planning to move in a few months. But you went and spoiled all that. You looked like you was gonna shoot me with that pig gun. That's why I ran. You're always shootin' and killin' us blacks! But Black Lives Matter. I know it means nothin' to you. So you goes and shoots my baby girl, Tswana. I'm not sorry one bit that I shot two of you! I'd shoot the whole lot of you if it would bring back my baby girl. You just wait until I get these handcuffs off of me and I'm free, free at last. You'd better not be carrying your white pig baby anywhere around me, cuz I'm telling you – you know what I'm sayin' – that I'm gonna kill that ugly baby just as sure as you killed mine, you motherfuckers!

***

The two of them were loitering on a corner near a liquor store. That very liquor store had been robbed seven times in the previous six months, and I'm telling you those two looked like they were planning something. Laquesha had these shifty but arrogant eyes and a loud mouth with too much lip gloss. Her "fiancé" looked like a thug, with bad skin and scars on his cheeks. As for their "baby," it sure didn't look like no "baby." It looked like a bag of ammunition. I've seen plenty of blacks hiding tons of ammo in baby carriages and tons of other places. They wait until you approach, and then they pull out the ammo and guns and come after you. Don't tell me what I see and what I don't see! They're killers. You expect me to be all careful and to read them their Miranda rights and be all gentlemanly so that bullets won't melt in my mouth. You're not out there on the street. I am! Fuck you. I'm not gettin' killed because I listened to your bullshit and didn't protect myself.

You want crimes stopped, huh? Of course you do. Well, who's stoppin' them? Me, that's who!

Did you see what happened to the murder rate when we, the police, went on strike for a week and refused to enforce the law? The murder rate went through the roof, that's what. Yeah, yeah, blacks get targeted disproportionately and they get punished for drug crimes too much. But they still commit far more than their *share* of crimes, and then they act like they never do *one* little thing wrong! It's all racism, racism, racism! Bullshit!

Why don't I shoot them in the leg or the arm? What do you think I am, a sucker? Have you ever seen a snake you just wounded and didn't kill? It sinks its teeth into you, first chance it gets. And then you're dead – and stupid – because you were too chickenshit to do the job right in the first place. Believe me, no blacks are gonna shoot you in the back by surprise when you shoot to kill right off the bat. Are you listening? Sure, we may catch a baby in the crossfire by mistake sometimes, but so do *they,* and a lot more than we do, as a matter of fact. So don't tell me how to do my job, asshole, as long as you just sit back on your fat ass and let people like me do the shit jobs for you! Poor Trayvon Martin, my ass!

[That last piece doesn't seem all that "sweet." Is the old storyteller falling off the track?]

[Well, it's sweet if people at least now understand where others are coming from, right?]

DREADLOCKED

KIRKWOOD HAD SEEN the guy before. He lived in his car, it seemed, a rundown old Pinto that he parked next to the Target store because he didn't have to move as much that way. The guy was about thirty, although he was so soiled and scruffy he could have been ten years younger. He had a pinched face and he had dreadlocks though he was white, long, unsightly dreadlocks that left bald rows on his skull. He had just gotten out of his Pinto and was taking a leak next to it. He grinned sheepishly as Kirkwood went by but didn't stop peeing. "They won't let me use the restroom," he said, pointing at the Target.

Kirkwood didn't say anything, just trudged up the slight hill toward the tiny coffee shop where he usually had breakfast. He was short of breath and feeling his years. He forced himself to stand up straight.

Suddenly, he heard two voices shouting at each other. He looked back and saw the guy who lived in his Pinto shaking his fist at another man with dreadlocks, this one not white. "You motherfuck!" the black man was yelling. This man had apparently smashed Pinto Guy's rear window, in broad daylight, and taken some items out of the car, at the same time that white Pinto Guy was pissing in the street. "What did you call me!?" the non-white dreadlocked guy was saying.

"You broke my window and I'm standing right here!" Pinto Guy was outraged.

"Finders keepers," the thief said. He had his arms full of what looked like CDs and posters. He looked snarly and determined to keep his "find."

"That's my Rolling Stones collection!" Pinto Man kept screaming.

"Yeah, what are you gonna do about it, call the cops?" Other Dreadlocked Man taunted, "And how dare you expropriate my hair style!"

Suddenly, Pinto Man opened the passenger-side door of his car and yelled at somebody inside. After a few seconds, an old Malamute dog made its way off the passenger seat. The dog was faded brown and gray with those nasty, icy blue eyes and evidently deaf. It had been sleeping during the car break-in and hadn't heard anything.

Black Dreadlocked Man came around to the sidewalk and looked at the old dog. "I'm really scared of Fido there!" he scoffed.

"Thor, kill!" Pinto Man shouted, his bad teeth showing.

"I'll kick its ass if it takes one step toward me!" the unrepentant thief said. He turned and started to walk up the slight hill in the same direction that Kirkwood was headed, his arms still full of his booty. He dropped a CD, which bounced on the pavement. He didn't bother to pick it up.

The dog seemed to be waiting for a hand signal from Pinto Man, not able to hear anything. He wagged his long tail uncertainly.

"Thor, kill that fucking thief!" his owner yelled. This time, he pointed his whole hand at the fleeing culprit.

The dog took off after Black Dreadlocked Man and caught him near the parking exit of the Target store. They played tug of war, the dog's teeth tight into the arm of the man's coat. In no time, the Malamute had him down and jumped on his chest. Pinto Man was running toward the two of them as Kirkwood watched at the top of the incline. The thief tried to kick the dog and at one point managed to get him by the scruff of the neck and throw him to the side. But before he could completely stand up, the dog lunged at him again and sank its teeth into a cheek. It yanked back and forth until a chunk came loose and Black Dreadlocked Man screamed, putting both hands over the horrible wound.

"Drop it! Drop it!" Pinto Man ordered the Malamute, who dropped the piece of flesh. Kirkwood called 911 on his cell phone and waited until the police car arrived and took the dazed and bloody thief away. They also cited Pinto Man for illegal parking and confiscated his CD and posters collection. Pinto Man, more and more pissed now, told the Malamute that he could have the cheek meat lying on the sidewalk. Thor wolfed it down as Kirkwood went off for his croissant and coffee.

In what possible way is this a "sweet" story?

Well, a crime was solved without a trial, a thief captured red-handed, and a hungry, old, deaf dog got fed.

THE OTHER SCHEHERAZADE

THERE ONCE WAS a mighty caliph who had a vast empire, forty-five wives, two hundred concubines, thirteen palaces, each made of rubies and pearls (and these were natural pearls, not your store-bought, overly round, commercial ones). He was forty and happy, or reasonably so. He did suffer from that ache just below the surface of consciousness that says how deeply disappointing life is at its core despite everything.

He also could not sleep. He had his apothecaries to concoct potions, balms, salves, and "solutions" (of all types) and yet none of them worked. The caliph could not sleep more than one hour a night.

Then one day he heard about a woman named Scheherazade, who was said to have a special but unknown power. "Shall I send for her?" the caliph asked his numerous wives and concubines.

"Try it. Maybe you'll give us all a rest!" the Comfort Women said as one.

So the caliph sent for Scheherazade, who got on a donkey and rode to the largest of the palaces, where the caliph was waiting for her on his throne, which was made of gold, silver, and Formica. (The Formica gave the throne strength.)

"How can I athitht you, O Great Calith?" Scheherazade inquired. To his surprise, she was old, bent, snaggle-toothed, and unpleasant to look upon. She also had a monotonous voice and a lisp.

"I can barely sleep at night," the caliph said, "and when it comes to afternoon naps, even post-coital ones, I am hopeless. I can stuff myself with dates and fine breads and lamb fricasseed, baked, and even soaked in mint yogurt, and still I cannot sleep!"

"I believe I have an answer," said Scheherazade.

"And what is that?"

"Tonight, I will come to your bedchamber and reveal all to you," she said.

The caliph looked askance at Scheherazade. "No hanky-panky!" he warned. "You're not my type."

"I have other talents," she answered cryptically.

"I'm so tired I'll try almost anything," replied the caliph.

That night she did *not* show up at the caliph's bedchamber. His guards searched high and low for her – in the harems, in the hanging gardens, even in a nearby, seedy Motel 6, all to no avail.

However, the next day, Scheherazade showed up at the caliph's main court. Everyone was surprised. "Where were you last evening?" the caliph asked her. "I waited and waited, all without sleep."

"Postponement of pleasures is paramount!" she proclaimed.

"I command you to come tonight at ten o'clock. If you do not appear, I will have my people track you down and torture you with a thousand afflictions, taken from many cultures."

Scheherazade bowed but said nothing.

That evening, she appeared at the caliph's bedchamber.

"Do not let her in!" said the bedchamber attendants. "You can't trust her."

"I will give him precious sleep," she replied. "That sounds like she will poison him!" cried some. "She is a witch and a hag and will surely do our great caliph enormous harm!" They all ran around with their hair on fire.

"Leave us alone," Scheherazade said. "My powers only work when I work alone."

After much complaining and resisting, the many attendants of the caliph dispersed, most uttering with disconsolate yelps of unease.

When the two were finally alone in the caliph's bedchamber, he put on his silk pajamas (made by high-caste Mongolians) and got into his large canopied bed. Scheherazade, in a nightgown made of mere cotton and horsehair, sat at the edge of his bed.

"Okay," the caliph said, "what have you got for your caliph?"

"I have many tales to tell," she began, "each more bizarre than the last!"

"Proceed!" demanded the caliph.

Scheherazade lifted her arms over her head. "Once upon a time, there was a . . ."

The caliph closed his eyes and fell into a deep sleep at once and slept through the night for eight hours. Thereafter, night after night, Scheherazade began a story and her listener fell into a deep sleep at once. He was narrative-intolerant, it turned out. But he got much-needed rest and made wise decisions for years. And Scheherazade did not even have to "put out," in tale or in tail, even once.

Thus was the story of the other Scheherazade.

CLEANING LADY

THE DAY the Immigration Van came for the cleaning lady, Isabella, she had just about finished Kirkwood's place. From his wheelchair, he had asked her to wipe away cobwebs in several corners with the broom. She was very short, with lots of Indian DNA in her Mexican heritage, and had to stand on the step-stairs to reach the cobwebs. She was a sourpuss, overall, but hadn't stolen anything over the years, as far as he could tell. She wore a rosary, for some reason around her neck, and kissed it often.

He was sorry to see her being deported back to Old Mexico, he guessed. He would miss her bi-weekly cleaning visits and supposed he'd have to scrub the kitchen and bathroom floors and the toilet – nasty tasks indeed – all by himself now and from his wheelchair. He didn't have the energy to try to find another cleaning lady – and if he did, she might be deported, too. He had not really liked Isabella that much, even though she'd been working for him for nine years. She was garrulous on the phone in Spanish but reticent and even sullen in English. She also often left early, not staying for the supposedly agreed-upon three hours, yet paid well over the minimum wage, coming to work whenever she damn well felt like it. Although she didn't steal, she'd brought her youngest son early on, and he had broken a knob on the dresser and teased Kirkwood's cat. She'd brought the kid only that one time. Kirkwood had asked once, when he'd driven her somewhere, where she was from. He had hesitated, as a good liberal, to ask her before, thinking it impolite, but the air had been heavy between them on that ride. She snapped, "Where are *you* from?" in an accusatory tone that Kirkwood didn't like one little bit. "I'm from Detroit," he'd answered her.

So he wasn't entirely unhappy that the Immigration Van was coming for Isabella. He had called it himself, as a matter of fact, knowing that they (the ICE people) would find it easier to round her up if she was alone and not surrounded by her eleven children, all of whom were citizens.

"Bye," Kirkwood said when Isabella was finally subdued and put inside the van and giving him the greasy eyeball and the finger.

"I worked for you for nine years!" she yelled, showing her callused hands. He felt sorry for her, especially her bad horse teeth, which she obviously didn't have enough money to have fixed. The driver started up the van and started to drive away. God, I don't want to clean the toilet, especially from my wheelchair, Kirkwood thought. But it was too late now, and Isabella was off to the land of her birth. "You can have your old job back when you come back *legally*, Isabella!" he said, cupping his hands and yelling.

[Now you're not even trying to be sweet! said many to the Old Writer.]

[You have to clean the palate every once in a while, replied the Old Writer.]

FLESH AND BLOOD

IN HIS FORTIES, Kirkwood had a son by an "alliance." The "alliance" had been between his sperm, a lesbian, and an eyedropper. Enough detail? The son that resulted was huge and handsome. Then time went by and he became just huge. He was a kindly young man who tipped too much and bled for all sorts of causes that his father did not give two hoots for. Kirkwood attributed it to being raised by lesbians, but perhaps it was merely genetic. Many things were genetic, Kirkwood thought, and wondered why people beat themselves up for things that weren't even under their control. He looked at his own genetics in wonder. He was in his late seventies and, though arthritic, looked twenty-five years younger and could get sucked off any time he chose to go to the Woods where the Cocksuckers lived.

The son turned out to be straight. "What can you do?!" Kirkwood said with feigned resignation.

He was actually glad that his son was heterosexual. It would make his life easier, not easy, but *easier*.

Kirkwood also harbored homophobia in his heart, and he would have been upset if his son were effeminate or, worse yet, trans-something. Who wanted to put on a Brave Face and always have to say, "We love Joella just the way she sees herself, whatever that is this month"?

Kirkwood and his son got along well enough, with the usual holidays celebrated: Christmas, the Fourth of July, birthdays galore, even what they called Sperm Day, which was October 19, the day Kirkwood had shot his sperm into an artichoke jar (with a wide opening) and donated it to the mid-wife who carried it to the lesbian waiting to be inseminated in a van. It sounded almost like a Greek myth when you thought about it. The son, Joe, even had a tattoo of the eyedropper on his arm and one of the artichoke jar on his upper back. Kirkwood didn't care for tattoos and so didn't have any. He waxed enthusiastic about his son's tattoos, but actually he didn't like them, even though they were about *him*.

One time, when the boy was about eight, he had said to his father on a visit, "I don't even like you."

Kirkwood had bitten his tongue and stopped himself from saying, "I don't like you, either."

Lots of family members don't really "like" each other, as seems obvious to any objective onlooker, but they are stuck with each other for better or worse. If trading relatives were permitted, there would, no doubt, be a great deal of it.

The son had completed two years of college and was working as a delivery man and had hurt his back lifting things. His remedy was pain-killers and beer, too much beer. He had also played lots of rugby in his youth and now he had all sorts of broken bones and cartilage tears and you name it. His doctor had told Joe that, at thirty, he had the body of a sixty-five-year-old man. Whatcha gonna do? thought Kirkwood. What if my son dies before I do?

The son thought his father was too conservative and mean. He resisted the reading materials his father sent him through the mail. Kirkwood thought that if they agreed more on basic things, they would have liked each other more. People really only "like" other people who approve of what they do. They put up with the rest.

When Kirkwood was in the hospital with a terrible hip infection from an operation gone awry, he was surprised when his son called him every day. At least Joe has a sense of duty with all these calls, he thought. The cell phone connection was spotty, their words flying back and forth between the two states, both mentally filling in the words they couldn't actually hear.

"What's this about you requesting an End of Life form?" Joe was saying. There was more than a hint of accusation in his voice.

"I didn't want to live if I was going to have to be bed-ridden," Kirkwood answered.

"You can't go yet! You're not that old."

"It's my life," Kirkwood said.

"You put it up on your Facebook page," Joe said.

"I did?"

"You don't remember that?"

"Not really. I was pretty doped up."

"Sharlene saw it there." Sharlene was Joe's wife. She was always super-enthusiastic about everything. That made Kirkwood suspicious. He thought she probably hated lots of things and just wouldn't say so. She suffered from migraines. They were trying to have a child, had been trying for over a year.

"I posted it on Sharlene's Facebook timeline?"

"No, on mine. But she reads mine."

Kirkwood didn't like that accusatory tone that Joe had in his voice. It seemed that Joe was holding back from shouting. This isn't going well, Kirkwood thought. "I didn't mean for Sharlene to read it," he said defensively.

"She got very upset and cried all day and all night."

Kirkwood mulled that over. He barely knew Sharlene, had seen her maybe six times. He had seen pictures of food that she had cooked that she had posted on Facebook. "She cried?" he said, incredulous.

"You upset her by saying that you wanted to die."

"But I did want to die. If I could have pushed a button from my bed, I would have pushed it a hundred and fifty times."

"But Sharlene shouldn't have seen that." Joe's voice was seething.

"Maybe she shouldn't read your Facebook posts," Kirkwood said.

"But she loves you!" Joe said.

This was news to Kirkwood. How could she love him? They had barely spoken in their six meetings. "Oh, for God's sake! Sharlene loves me?!"

"And *I* love you!" Joe said. "And I don't want you to die, Dad."

"Yeah, you'd have to have those tattoos removed," Kirkwood joked.

"No, I'd keep them," Joe said. "And I will keep them until I die."

Both their voices caught in their throats.

"I never knew how much I loved you until you went into the hospital," Joe said, his voice catching.

Kirkwood couldn't stop the tears welling in his eyes. His voice catching too, he finally he managed to say, "I'm sorry if I made Sharlene cry. I didn't mean to . . . And I don't want to die anymore. Not since you called. Not since you called, son."

CHIRPS

IN THE DIALYSIS CENTER, the smoke detector had been chirping every forty-five seconds for three whole days. "It needs a new battery. It's been years," said somebody – the Assistant Manager, Fat Jerry, who was good with his hands. He had even managed, with great difficulty and danger, to stand on a wobbly chair and unscrew the cover of the smoke detector. Inside, it seemed to be all electrical wires and no battery. "Do you see where the battery goes?" Ancient Gus asked. Gus was fifty but looked seventy-five.

"I'm looking. I'm looking," Jerry said, sweating in his armpits and afraid he would fall off the chair and break something.

"*I* need a new battery too!" said Riza, who was also ancient and from the Philippines and wore hats. She was a corker.

"I can't see a place for any battery!" Jerry complained. "I don't have a fresh battery, anyway."

"Anybody got a spare battery?" Ancient Gus asked.

There was a new chirp over Jerry's big head. "Damn that noise!" he swore.

"Well, at least it's still alive," Riza said. Then she laughed until she got a stitch in her side.

All the other patients at the Dialysis Center more or less woke up and looked at the smoke detector. There were twenty-two of them, sitting in wheelchairs for the most part. They all had terminal kidney problems and looked like old turtles. Of course, the chair that Jerry was standing on broke, throwing him to the hard linoleum floor.

He finally got up but was hobbling. "Jesus H. Christ!" he swore. "I think I may have cracked a bone in my leg."

"Don't use the Lord's name in vain!" Ancient Gus snapped. "Especially around Christmas." He pointed at the wreaths the staff had put up, one on the outside door, the other on the door to the treatment room.

"It's Christmastime. It's not in vain," Fat Jerry snapped right back.

"It's the *holiday* season, not just Christmas," said Laser Billy, who usually didn't say all that much while the patients awaited their turns.

Somebody came in from outside, making the cold wind blow through the place. It was the angry, burly, cranky man who lived around the corner. "Your van driver is blocking the street outside – again!" Angry-Burly-Cranky was always bitching about the center's van blocking cars outside. He was red-faced and murderous-looking. It had been because of him that Fat Jerry had put up the NO GUNS ALLOWED sign posted on the glass section of the front door, right below the Seasonal Wreath.

"Wait till you're in here with your kidneys all shot! Then you won't complain about the van!" That was what Riza thought.

"I'll never wind up in here! I'll shoot myself first," the angry, burly, cranky man said. "After I shoot the whole bunch of you losers!"

All the old turtles mumbled various ethnic curses at him.

"Are you gonna move the goddamned van or not?" The angry, burly, cranky man did not wait for an answer and went out onto the sidewalk and confronted the van driver as she was wheeling in another turtle. Nobody inside could hear the words being exchanged, but both the driver's and Angry-Burly-Cranky's mouths were going a mile a minute. The van driver was a Black and Proud woman of color with street creds coming out of her ass for days. Angry-Burly-Cranky was no match for her, and in no time at all she had knocked him silly with one fist and then run over his ankle with the wheelchair, leaving him screaming. The old turtle that she was bringing in was so far gone he slept through it all. Meanwhile, the smoke detector kept on chirping. It was maddening.

"Who's got a gun?" Fat Jerry asked the room. "I'll shoot the damn thing and that'll shut it up!" His fat face was covered with fat sweat.

Near the entrance and inside now, out of the cold, the female van driver was saying to the angry, burly, cranky and screaming man that she had run over, "I'm sorry! I'm sorry!" You could tell that she wasn't sorry, but she was afraid of a lawsuit. She was also afraid he might have a gun. She had one, too, but it was out in the van.

The neighbor's ankle, it turned out, wasn't broken. Even the skin wasn't. He was wearing some sort of heavy sock for diabetics. "I'm going to sue you for millions!" he was yelling as he hopped around.

"Oh, get over your white privilege!" Riza was yelling.

"She deliberately ran over my ankle! Thank God for my diabetes!" the man said. "I have diabetes privilege! Fuck you, you ugly old turtle!"

They all went on screaming and yelling and cursing until the Manager of the facility came out of his inner sanctum and looked stern. He had a commanding presence and wore very nice suits. "Do you want me to shut this Tower of Babel down today and send you all home *without* your dialysis?" Everybody settled down after that, and the Manager went back into his inner sanctum. They awaited their turns for treatment, the Assistant Manager got a fresh white shirt from his office, and there was no lawsuit or gun battle. Riza had made some homemade eggnog and poured cups from a thermos. It turned out that the man from around the corner was an electrician, and those who could stood around him as he stood on a chair – a sturdy one – and the rest cheered him on and toasted him with eggnog as he opened the smoke detector, then re-wired it so that it didn't need a battery, and it stopped its horrible chirp, and the old turtles were happy (even though the eggnog was forbidden, maybe *because* it was forbidden), and they all got their dialysis and lived through that Christmas – *every one.*

ELF VS. SANTA

SANTA CLAUS, round and jolly though he was, did not think Akmed on the outskirts of Cairo should get any gifts for Christmas. Merry Merry Elf, one of Santa's helpers, thought otherwise. Merry Merry Elf was a bleeding heart. She was dressed in a darling little green cap that accented her pointy ears and sweet little mouth to a fare-thee-well.

"He can't help it if he's a Muslim," said Merry Merry Elf.

"Yes, he can!" shouted Santa Claus. "He can renounce his faith."

"But he'll be killed if he does that," said Merry Merry.

"I won't reward bad behavior!" Santa looked adamant. "Akmed stoned a transsexual to death."

"It's very hard to give up the religion you are born into." Merry Merry looked quite contrary. "Especially if you are killed for leaving."

"You don't need any religion at all," said Santa. "Look at me. I am an atheist and I still give out millions of presents every year."

"I still don't know how you manage to get all those gifts in one sleigh," Merry Merry said. "You are amazing."

"Don't try to compliment me into giving Akmed a Christmas present!" Santa bellowed.

Merry Merry put down the long roll of paper with the recipients' names on it. "I don't know if I can work for you anymore, Santa," she said.

"What?!" Santa exclaimed. "It's not as if we haven't disagreed before on who's naughty or nice."

"Yes, but you always gave in before."

"The last time I remember us fighting like this was over O.J. Simpson. You finally realized that that murderer did not deserve presents!" Santa tossed a Chevy Malibu into his sleigh.

"He *was* found *not guilty* by a jury of his peers." The Elf shook her pointy head.

"The man was guilty as hell. He killed his ex-wife and her male friend – slashed them to death!"

"But he was a person of color!"

"Oh, for Christ's sake," Santa grumbled.

"It's better to sin on the side of forgiveness." Merry Merry looked quite smug with righteousness.

"No, the season is about *justice*!" Santa snapped. "The nice are rewarded; the naughty are punished. And this year, at last, I'm putting my foot down."

"But is anyone ever really guilty of anything?" asked Merry Merry. "Everyone should walk in others' shoes."

"You don't see the crimes I see! Sometimes people steal my milk and cookies right out of my hands!"

"They must be very hungry."

"Last year one kid stabbed one of my reindeer in the throat. I just didn't tell you."

"He must have been a Laplander, then, and needed sustenance."

"Like hell he was! He was just a mean kid."

"Did you ask him to say he was sorry?"

"No, I ran over him with the sleigh."

"You killed him?"

"I tried, but he was a tough little turd."

"Santa, what has been happening to you of late? You seem to find more naughty than nice."

"Maybe it's because there *are* more naughty than nice! In fact, there have always been more naughty than nice!"

"I think people are just misunderstood. Basically, they are good at heart."

"What universe are you living in? More people get away with things than ever get caught!" screamed Santa. "Who travels the world every year and sees the kind of shit people pull? Me, that's who! You just stay here in my workshop, living in your fantasy world about no evil in the world. I see it! I live it! But I try to protect you from it. You have it too cozy here. You need to get outside and see what's what!"

Merry Merry Elf began to cry. "I don't want to go outside, Santa. Please don't make me. And don't tell me the bad stuff."

"Why, you afraid of the truth, Pointy Head?" Santa said, baring his teeth. "You afraid of the truth? Huh? You afraid of the *truth*?!"

"Yes. I don't think I can go on making toys for people if I know the truth, as you report it."

Santa needed Merry Merry Elf for his workforce, so he gave in, again, and brought Akmed on the outskirts of Cairo a new prayer rug. But one with rocks in it to make his knees hurt when he thanked Allah for allowing him to stone transsexuals.

BARNYARD

THE TURKEYS on Rancher Brown's turkey farm decided to hold an election for Head Turkey. Just because. Most of the turkeys were not interested in politics and very few read a newspaper or watched cable television. They hung around the grain trough, displaying their wattles, snoods, and caruncles, and gobbled about the Liberal Bias in the air.

"They're all crooked," said one hen about politics.

"So true," clucked another.

They both chased a cricket across a ditch, but it got away.

"I may not even vote!" bragged Tom Turkey, his red snood wiggling back and forth.

Nevertheless, the election was on. Two major candidates quickly grabbed the spotlight. One was an old, bald hen from the Establishment – a line of turkeys (named Turkey) that went way back. She was not much liked on the ranch, but she was persistent and well-financed. She promised the turkeys everything under the sun, including the sun. She started out as a bad gobbler, but as the months of the election campaign wore on, she got better.

The other major candidate was named Big Cock, an overweight, randy, orange-combed male who had more self-esteem than was warranted. He would leap up onto a tree stump at every opportunity and gobble and carry on until the sun set. He ran a negative campaign, saying that there were dark-meat turkeys on the next farm who were trying to horn in on Rancher Brown's ranch and take grain from their trough. He said everything would be big and wonderful under his guidance.

There were several minor candidates for the position of Head Turkey, but they were dispatched in a series of debates before the assembled flock. Big Cock got rid of most of them by assigning them insulting names like Little Cock and Low-Energy and Ugly-Neck. People laughed at the rude names and voted in the primaries for Big Cock. They thought he was "authentic."

The old, bald hen of the rival party, whose name was Miriam Rodham Turkey, called Big Cock's constituents a Nest of Unadorables and received much outrage as a result. She apologized and said she meant to say "a Nest of Adorables" but had misspoken. It is not well known, yet quite true, that turkeys do not like to be called Unadorables.

Big Cock also said some things that irritated his opponents, but he would not apologize, ever. When he accused Miriam Rodham Turkey of giving secret gobbling for stacks and stacks of grain, his supporters accepted his charges against the old hen and started yelling "CHOP HER HEAD OFF!" at rallies. Some said that Big Cock was bringing up allegations against his main opponent to distract from his own unseemly behavior. Several young hens had come forward and accused Big Cock of grabbing their wattles without their consent while chewing breath mints to hide his turkey breath. He denied the charges and threatened to sue the young hens after the election. "I'm a thoroughly upstanding cock!" he maintained.

Big Cock's lovely wife, who was imported from a turkey ranch in Moldova, stood by her husband and gave several endorsements inside the barn. She gobbled in a thick accent and thus was hard to understand, but everyone agreed that she had lovely wattles. Their child, an impassive jake, stood by his mother's side and paid no attention and never smiled or clucked. Big Cock, sensing a slip in his ratings, declared that he was going to build a wall around the ranch to keep the dark-meat turkeys out and to deport any found on Rancher Brown's land without papers. Rancher Brown rarely figured in the lives of the turkey residents since he lived in a big house across the yard. But they did notice that some of their numbers regularly disappeared at certain times of the year. The turkeys referred to these as the Bad Times and did not like to speak of them. There was one word in particular they all agreed never to say aloud: *Thanksgiving*. It was rumored that ritual slaughter occurred at that time, even festive chewing on the turkeys' very flesh. It was so unbelievably cruel and hideous most of the turkeys would not believe it. Most thought even to bring up the subject made it more likely to be true.

The poults did not pay any attention at all to the election campaign. They even mocked it and said they couldn't vote and so they were not going to pay any attention. They wouldn't have paid attention even if they could have voted.

The turkeys didn't know who exactly was leading the race, but they did do an informal poll and found that Miriam Rodham Turkey seemed to be ahead. She agreed to three debates with Big Cock in three different locations on the property after he complained that he was not getting enough coverage.

In the first debate, it was generally agreed by the gobblers and hens who watched it, that Miriam Rodham Turkey won, primarily because Big Cock kept bringing up topics like how disgusting she was because she took a long bathroom break and that an uncle of hers had once worked in Washington D.C. "as an assassin for Rosie O'Duck." She kept her cool, smiled a lot, and shuddered her feathers when Big Cock went all macho on her.

The second debate was more even, because Big Cock acted more "Presidential." That is, he only twice said he was going to put her in prison after he won and used a handkerchief instead of spewing his turkey phlegm on her old, bald head.

In the third debate, Big Cock said he was going to bring Heaven to the ranch in a big box with a pretty ribbon on top and kept interrupting Miriam Rodham Turkey with the word "Wrong" whenever she recited facts and figures about health care and education. She had been advised not to look "too un-henlike" no matter what he said, so she didn't pluck his eyes out, the way she wanted to.

More allegations against Big Cock came out after the debates, saying that he would have business conflicts of interest if he were elected. He found an old iPhone in the weeds and opened a Twitter account and starting sending out allegations of his own. He claimed that Miriam Rodham Turkey was "rapacious" and "lesbacious" and that she allowed spies from nearby ranches to read her scribblings in the dirt around her roost. She denied everything.

Miriam Rodham Turkey responded by saying that Big Cock had a "known hair stylist" who fluffed up his orange comb "on a regular basis" and was temperamentally unfit to be Head Turkey because of his flare-ups. Big Cock's supporters scoffed at these allegations and went blind with rage whenever Big Cock was accused of anything except brilliance. "He's goddamned authentic!" they clucked.

Scuffles broke out in rallies and gatherings on both sides now. The turkeys were riled up and looking for red meat, though they usually had preferred fruits and berries before. One poult lost an eye when it got in the way of two angry opponents. Rancher Brown thought he heard some commotion out in the yard, but he didn't care much and didn't investigate.

Finally, the election itself came. Turkeys lined up early at the one polling booth, the outhouse behind the barn. They each dropped a pellet from their hind quarters into a wooden bucket and made their scratch in the dirt. It took the voting committee a long time to count the pellets, because they weren't always legible or dry, and none of the counters was very bright. Some arguments about which votes to discard erupted, and the squawking went on throughout the night.

At last came the tally. Miriam Rodham Turkey won the popular vote. Big Cock won the Electoral College vote. "It's all rigged! What's the Electoral College?" Big Cock cried foul.

"But you won. You're now Head Turkey!" shouted his supporters.

"Oh, I am?" said Big Cock. "So I guess it's not rigged after all! Now let's build that wall and drain the swamp!"

"How could Big Cock have possibly won?!" cried Miriam Rodham Turkey's supporters. "He was losing in the polls, he lies, and he tweets like he's insane!"

Never, never underestimate the power of Resentment in the underbird. That, boys and girls, is how democracy works.

Among turkeys.

METHANE ESCAPE

WHEN KIRKWOOD was a boy, he was raised Catholic. That meant that every morning, he would get up at seven A.M. on his own – his mother and father liked to sleep in. Sitting in his bow tie and Husky-Size trousers, cute little face all aglow, he would have cold cereal with milk and hot cocoa, then gather his school things, and walk the ten minutes to school. Or rather to Mass. Attendance at Mass was mandatory five days a week at eight A.M., to say nothing of Sunday. Kirkwood was a devout believer in what he had been taught and was never late, not once. He was even an altar boy on certain days, although to tell the truth he did not like saying the responses to the priest – in Latin, this was. He didn't know what anything meant and was shocked to learn that Requiem Masses had different responses for the altar boys. Some of the priests looked askance at him when he said the wrong Latin words. He also didn't like having to ring the bell during the elevation of the Host. At his church, the "bell" was actually a gong that required five notes, and Kirkwood was such a sensitive, nervous boy that he always made sure he was on the celebrating priest's left side because it was the altar boy on the right who had to sound the gong. He had never had to sound the gong.

A lot was said about *SIN* both in the church and in the classroom, and Kirkwood accepted it all, largely because he heard no other points of view. He could tell you when a venial sin became a Mortal and when a Fallopian pregnancy might be terminated – never. He prayed for the souls in Purgatory and felt guilty the one time he accidentally left a fragment of the Host on the railing of the pew where he was kneeling after receiving Holy Communion. He had drooled Our Lord's Body and Blood on that railing and was convinced into a sweaty confrontation with his conscience that maybe it was *NOT* an accident and that he had

MEANT to do it. It took three Confessions of that particular act to ease his anxiety.

By the time he got to senior year in high school, Kirkwood had begun to question some of the dogmas of the Church. How could somebody be a sacrifice on a cross for other people's sins? It seemed like something from the Dark Ages. Kirkwood had read about the Dark Ages in a book. Sometimes, he wondered if he was also living in the Dark Ages. He thought about telling the priest in Confession about his doubts but decided not to. Having Doubts was probably a *SIN* all by itself.

Still, it was not the doubts about what was a sin and what wasn't that changed Kirkwood's life forever, not even the Sexual Thoughts that now kept creeping into his thoughts – filthy thoughts and acts that were meant only for Someone You Loved!

No, what changed him and ultimately saved him was the seating/praying arrangement of the church he attended every morning at eight A.M. The boys' pews were on one side of the center aisle; the girls' pews were on the other side. As each boy arrived for Mass, he would slide into the next open spot. Usually Kirkwood was the first or second boy to arrive, and so he would be in the first row of pews. Other boys would fill in behind him. But somewhere along the line (October 14, 1955), he found himself feeling very gaseous as he got on the kneeler to pray. He wasn't sure how stinky the odor was, but he thought it was pretty strong. He wasn't quite sure what methane smelled like, yet maybe this was it. He had smelled cow methane on his uncle's farm in Illinois, and it was not pleasant. He rested his butt on the seat with his knees still on the kneeler. Maybe he could keep the methane inside that way. He found himself very pained trying not to issue any more.

But in the row behind him, he heard Raymond Kowalski whispering to Anthony Carbone: "I think it's Kirkwood," he said, snickering. "Whew!" Anthony Carbone said. He laughed even harder than Raymond Kowalski.

Kirkwood flushed to the roots of his hair. And the next day, he deliberately arrived late for Mass, knowing that, if he did, he would be in the last row of the pews for the boys. There he would have no one behind him who could smell his methane. No matter what he did now, he couldn't stop the morning silent explosions. Maybe it was the cocoa. Or his teenaged body. Or whatever. He even prayed to God for the methane to stop, but it didn't.

Coming later and later to Mass led to questioning the Virgin Birth and the prohibition against masturbation. One doubt led to yet another, even to his asking the nuns to be relieved of his duties as an altar boy, and before long, by his first year in college, Kirkwood was out of that big cult known as the Catholic Church and out of the Dark Ages. And every day, he thanked the Great Nobody in the sky for the farts that had saved him.

IMPULSES

A "FRIEND" of Kirkwood's and Kirkwood had never met in person although they were "friends" on a website. The "friend," who lived in a housing project, was not having a good time of it. He suffered from macular degeneration, limiting his vision to the narrow periphery of each eyeball. He was eighty years old and one leg had grown shorter than the other through one disease or another. He lived alone except for his one surviving basset hound, Baggley. He loved Baggley and fed him and hugged him, but the dog paid less and less attention to him, growing deaf and blind and crippled. Four pre-teen boys in the housing project were also mean to Baggley's owner and teased and taunted him whenever they saw him. They threw rocks at him and called him a faggot. One of them even took off his belt and swiped at Baggley's jowls and hit the dog hard on the nose. They thought they were hot shit. They were only half-right.

Baggley's owner confessed on his private message board to having strange impulses. When he was at the Food Bank, he suddenly wanted to reach out and grab women and thrust his penis into them. He wasn't even a little bit heterosexual, so he found this impulse very odd. He imagined men and women having sex in the shopping carts at the Kroger store he sometimes went to and wanted to join them. He said, "I had to slap myself across the jaw three times yesterday to stop myself from getting in a shopping cart." He wondered if he had Alzheimer's. He'd had some scans done at a free clinic, and they showed plaque and amyloids, or something like that. Somehow, his records got mis-filed and he forgot to ask any more about his results.

Meanwhile, the impulses continued. He peed in the fish pond, right through the fence that was meant to protect the one remaining goldfish that had managed so far to escape the rocks of the mean boys. The goldfish was found floating upside down two days after Kirkwood's "friend" had peed in the pond. He felt sure that he had killed it.

He was petting a stray cat on a grim November day without sunshine and suddenly kicked it for no reason except that it seemed too needy and its purr was too loud. It limped away. "But I love animals!" the man said. He sat in his one-bedroom apartment with the broken heater and cried. He had a corn dog as a special treat, but he gagged on it, got mad, tore off the rest of the corn dog and jabbed the pointed stick into his shorter leg. "I just wanted to!" he marveled. "It still hurts and it may be infected."

Kirkwood was busy with something, so he only had time to **LIKE** Baggley's owner's posting on the website. He added a smiley face. It didn't seem appropriate, but what else could he do? He and his "friend" lived a thousand miles apart.

Then Kirkwood didn't see any more postings from his "friend" and was afraid the next thing he would hear is that he had passed away and some relative was shutting down the man's web-page. What he did hear was even worse: "Kerry Louis Poppe, 80, was found in his public housing apartment in an apparent murder-suicide with his companion and best friend, Baggley, a basset hound thought to be about 14 years old. A shotgun was found near the bodies, but there was no note."

Just kidding!

Kirkwood's "friend" actually won the Super Lotto, got his own mansion, excellent health coverage, was cured of his eye problems, as well as his short leg, and he and Baggley lived to be one hundred and eighty-nine years old and died in their sleep in each other's arms.

[Sweet, sweet enough?]

ENDANGERED

WHEN KIRKWOOD was a boy of nine, he had a special pet, a real miniature elephant. It was about the size of a Golden Retriever, only gray, small-eyed, and hard to hold for very long. Its trunk was somewhat crooked, veering off to the right and was always searching for food even though Bloopy (as he was called) was well fed. Bloopy had hard hair bristles that grew on his back and hurt the hand that dared to pet him. Kirkwood's parents, Lola and Boyd, didn't want Bloopy to live in the house because he knocked things off tables and shelves and deposited dung in the oddest places.

Kirkwood, a sensitive boy (and we all know what that means now), loved Bloopy very much. For one thing, he was the only child in the neighborhood who had a pet elephant. The others had dogs and cats and the occasional bird. He would visit with Bloopy out in the backyard and brush his bristles with a brush and even take naps with him in the "elephant house" that Boyd and Lola had built for their son's pet. (Lola had contributed to the building of the "elephant house" every bit as much as her husband had and was even better at construction, it goes without saying, as she was an early feminist.)

One day, the family decided to take Bloopy to a pet-grooming service. His toenails were becoming a problem, as were his rapidly growing tusks. There they would have everything trimmed. Once they were all in the pet-grooming store – Bloopy in his little elephant cage with the proper air vents – they made a joint family decision to have the groomer trim the bristles on Bloopy's back as well. They stuck up quite prominently and were downright sharp.

The groomer came out of the back with a big, warm smile on his face. He had red hair and freckles and a grooming license on the rear wall. (Actually, he was Guatemalan with pitted, dark skin, no grooming license whatsoever, and with no green card and no smile, but you can't say that.)

They discussed the price for the grooming services, and all agreed that it sounded reasonable.

The groomer (Mr. Sean) smoochy-cooed Bloopy through the air vents in the cage and then lifted it up and said, "He's quite the big boy!" referring to Bloopy's weight. Bloopy did not know where he was being taken and didn't like it and trumpeted several times.

"It'll be all right," Kirkwood soothed in his little-boy voice.

The family took seats in the waiting room and read magazines and also had ice-cold water from a big upside-down bottle in the corner. They felt refreshed.

After half an hour, the groomer (Mr. Sean) came out of the back with Bloopy in the cage. His toenails, tusks, and bristles had been trimmed, and he looked great. The family went home and ordered Chinese take-out and even gave Bloopy some and let him sleep in Kirkwood's bed that night because he was frightened from his trip to the pet groomers.

The End

[It's sweet, but there's no story there. It's supposed to be sweet STORIES.]

When the groomer (Manuel Jose) came out of the back of the grooming shop, he was carrying Bloopy's dead body in his arms. Manuel was short and Bloopy's trunk was long. So it dragged on the floor. Manuel was no longer smiling. "What happened to Bloopy?" young Kirkwood cried out.

Lola and Boyd ran to their boy and covered his eyes and ears. They were Americans and didn't want their offspring to experience something bad, ever.

"Bloopy just collapsed on the grooming table," Manuel said.

He was obviously lying. There were bruises on Bloopy's head as well as two cracked ribs sticking out of his left side.

"What have you done to Bloopy?!" Kirkwood asked in his little-gay voice.

"Your pet elephant got out of hand!" Manuel said, in broken English. (Which cannot be phonetically spelled out here, as that would be "racist.")

"So you beat Bloopy?!" Kirkwood's parents exclaimed as one. (They agreed on most things and did not like to argue in front of their son.)

"Your elephant slapped me with his trunk!" Manuel replied. "Nobody slap Manuel!" He thrust Bloopy's body into Kirkwood's arms and ran out of the grooming store. He disappeared into the great Fabric of American Society and was never heard of again. He became a legal citizen ten years later, felt belated remorse, and visited Bloopy's gravesite at the pet cemetery every Sunday.

The End

[Jesus, what do you want from me? That's a sweet ending!]

[Okay, how about this:]

When Manuel brought Bloopy out of the back of the grooming shop, the poor miniature elephant was gasping for breath. "Help him!" Manuel cried. "Help him! I can't!" Both Kirkwood's parents (Lola and Boyd) tried mouth-to-mouth resuscitation on Bloopy, but he panicked and kept hitting them with his trunk. They had no choice but to back off.

Then Kirkwood, the nine-year-old, non-cynical version of himself, began giving his friend Bloopy mouth-to-mouth. Because Bloopy knew his friend well and had always been treated as an equal, not a pet that somebody "owned," he let the boy blow air into him. That air saved that miniature elephant's life. And that night, they went home and ordered a pizza for the four of them: extra-large with peanuts.

The End

[Okay, okay, the illegal alien (sorry, the undocumented, hard-working, soon-to-be-citizen) Manuel actually not only did the grooming (perfectly) but gave Bloopy perfect mouth-to-mouth resuscitation and saved that otherwise endangered miniature elephant.]

[Satisfied?]

[We have more taboos than the Victorians!]

I'M GOING TO KILL YOUR BABY

"HELLO. I'm going to kill your baby," the stranger announced.

"You're going to kill my baby?" I said.

"Are you hard of hearing?"

"No."

"Then don't repeat the obvious."

"I thought maybe you said something else."

"How many other things sound like 'I'm going to kill your baby'?"

"But you can't mean what you said."

"Oh, but I do!"

I clutched my baby to my breast, making it squall. "Hush," I said.

"You have a noisy baby."

"Is that why you're going to kill it?"

"No."

" . . . Are you going to give me a reason?"

"No."

I clutched my baby even harder. I pulled the baby blanket over its eyes. I felt vulnerable standing there in the rain, the droplets smashing against my forehead, nose, chin, collar, shoulders, and back.

"You'd better hand over your baby to me," the stranger demanded. It was a woman, I think, large and powerful and cruel of eye.

I thought that if I engaged the stranger in conversation I might save my baby. "Are you barren yourself, and that's made you bitter and angry?" I asked. "Perhaps you just want to *kidnap* my baby and raise it as your own?"

"If I was, do you think I'd want your baby of all the babies I could kidnap? Get over yourself! There's nothing special about either of you."

"Oh," I muttered, covering my baby's ears. I did not want its self-esteem injured, especially at such an early age.

"Besides, don't you know the statistics on adoptions?! Most of them are disastrous."

"What do you mean?" I asked.

"You don't know what *disastrous* means?! It means that if the adopted babies don't turn on the adoptive parents and make their lives miserable, they murder them in their bed and set their corpses on fire."

"Really? That does sound disasterous. I've never read that."

"It's *disastrous* – you drop the 'e'. You ought to read more." The stranger snorted in contempt.

"You sound very smart," I said.

"The orphanages hide the facts from the public so that they'll keep on adopting." The large, womanly stranger took a threatening step toward me.

"I think I'll be stepping away now," I said.

"No, you won't," she said. "I won't let you." She pulled a machete out of the very large Gucci handbag she was holding. Obviously stolen – the handbag, not the machete.

I didn't know what to do. The rain was still pouring down. What if I tried to run and slipped and fell and dropped and killed my baby? What if I confronted the stranger and tried to look big, as one does with a grizzly bear or a mountain lion? That might work. On the other hand, that could allow the stranger time to cut my baby in half with the machete.

So there I stood in the vicious rain facing a vicious stranger who wanted to kill my poor, helpless baby. What should I do? What should I do?!

You ever heard of "The Lady or the Tiger"? Well, this is one of those stories. *You* have to choose the ending.

Okay. A little help.

1) The stranger swung the machete at the narrator, but because of the slippery conditions, she slipped as she swung and cut off her own head. The narrator and the baby escaped.

2) The narrator rushed the vicious stranger and held her down until a passerby called 911. Eventually, "they" got help for the poor, benighted woman and she became a fire-woman and saved many babies from many fires.

3) The baby sensed the danger from the stranger and, although just seven months old, spoke its first word: HELP! Only in Spanish. A passing police patrol car heard the word and, with the help of a passing unarmed black man, rescued the baby and its single parent, got the stranger some help, and they met every year thereafter on November 4 to rejoice and tightly hug each other in this vicious world.

[Fake!?]

[Fake is better than nothing!]

THE UNHAPPY CAT

EGREGIOUS was an eleven-year-old Siamese who was not happy.

First of all, he wasn't pleased that he had been named after a non-existent Roman emperor by his smart-Alec staff – or "owner" as the man referred to himself. A retired history professor. Big deal, Egregious thought. At least most people didn't know what "egregious" means and didn't call him by his name anyway. They just said, "Shoo!" and "Get out!" when they saw him on "their" property. Some of them even petitioned the Board of the condo complex where he and the retired professor lived, saying that dog owners were required to "pick up after" their dogs, but cat "owners" were allowed to let their cats pee and poop wherever they felt like it, and it had to stop. Try and stop me! thought Egregious. At least I cover mine up. Those filthy dogs just dump and leave it!

Egregious was also unhappy that the new pet door in the back bedroom was smaller than the previous one. He could barely squeeze through it. His "owner" also stuck his cigarette butts in the litter box near the pet door, the litter box that Egregious had used once, in an emergency. Those cigarette butts smelled terrible, unlike the lovely weeds out back or Mary Jane's butt. Mary Jane, a calico, was the other cat who lived in the condo. Egregious rarely paid attention to Mary Jane, except to smell her butt now and again and open his mouth and show his teeth as he drank in the odor. Mary Jane was a suck-up and spent too much time on the old professor's lap. She always got the better bowl of food, too, at their twice-daily feedings, no matter what the professor claimed about equal treatment. When it came to the birds out in the holly bushes behind the condo, they were no fun at all. They got all fluttery and jittery when Egregious so much as sat on the fire escape and looked at them.

He just wanted to play tag with them, but, *no*, not them!

The mice were even worse. They wouldn't even say hello. They got all quiet and hidey when Egregious merely stretched out on the fire escape. They were also clannish.

He had met a nice big brown rat named Boss a few years prior, but something must have happened to him and he didn't come around anymore. Fuck him! Egregious thought.

And as for the food the retired professor put out, he never seemed to know the right amount to leave. A lot of it wound up with yucky mold on top. "Fancy Feast, my ass!" Egregious swore. "Who'd eat such crap?! Nobody but Mary Jane, apparently. Fuck her, too!"

Once in a while, Egregious would stay out all night. It was boring for the most part, but it worried the retired professor, and that was sort of fun. But then Egregious would get scolded for staying out all night. What am I – two months old?! he scoffed. One night he stole somebody's old sanitary napkin from a garbage can, just to have something to do.

There were some coyotes who had migrated from outside the city across a bridge and settled just a few blocks from Egregious's condo. Word on the street was that they had killed a Maine Coon on Plymouth Rock Road and mauled a puppy on Dewdrop Lane. Egregious was pretty sure he had seen two of the coyotes one foggy night. They looked skinny and hungry. You couldn't be too careful. He had intimated to the professor to get a .22 and shoot the suckers, but the man was a big baby and said, "Our coyotes are native species and were here before we were." How do you get territory? You *take* it, that's how! Jesus Christ! What a pussy! thought Egregious.

He yawned a lot. He scratched at the fleas that loved his fur. He watched a spider build a web near the ceiling of the study, then ate it. Egregious was still unhappy.

Then one Christmas, among the catnip and the plastic mice and other junk that the old professor had bought for Egregious was another present. He had no idea what it was, but he ripped off the wrapping and ribbon with his claws and teeth and revealed an envelope. Inside was a gift certificate and a CD from a veterinarian downtown. It read: "A SECOND CHANCE IN LIFE."

It turned out to be a new form of surgery especially tailored to unhappy cats. It was all very tastefully presented and Egregious was intrigued. He watched the video twice and made an appointment through the professor and on December 28, his twelfth birthday, he had the operation. Through the magic of microsurgery, the vet replaced both testicles that had been removed from Egregious when he was a kitten, without his consent needless to say.

And because of those wonderful new Christmas balls – don't ask where they came from, boys and girls – he was no longer an unhappy cat as he roamed the night, every night.

ASYLUM?

(In a play version, this was first published in *World Literature Review* and then performed in *Fest of the Best* at Lama Theater, NYC, April 2016.)

LEONA WAS completing some forms. She perused one and then put it aside, unable to make up her mind what to do with it. She waved her hand at the form as if to say, "I'll get back to you." Leona was forty, portly, and always professionally dressed for work, her graying hair upswept, and with just a hint of makeup. She was thinking about having that mole beside her nose removed.

There was a knock at the office door.

"Yes?"

Outside, a voice, in broken English, said, "I have appointment."

Leona got up, went to the door, and opened it. "Come in, won't you?" She smiled.

"Thank you, thank you!" said the man who entered the room. He looked to be about twenty-seven, very humble, very nervous, ingratiating, smiling too much. He was dressed in several layers of dark clothing, several coats and sweaters, even two pairs of pants. He had stubble on his lower face. His eyes were fierce.

Leona pointed. "Have a seat, won't you?"

"Yes, yes, thank you so much." He took the chair farthest from her.

"No, sit closer, please," she said.

"Are you sure? They usually don't want us to . . ."

"It's fine."

"Okey-dokey then!" the man said, overly jovial as he took the chair closer to her.

"Do you have your immigration form?"

"Oh, yes, yes." The man searched himself and found the form in his coat pocket. "I'm sorry it is wrinkled. I got … "

Leona smiled at him. "Not a problem. I've seen worse."

The man handed over the immigration form.

Leona looked it over. "You filled it out yourself?"

"Yes, yes!"

"Your English is quite good."

"Oh, no, terrible, terrible English. I apologize."

"No need to apologize. Believe me, I've seen terrible English."

"I try! I try very hard! The English is not easy."

"You're right. My parents were immigrants. They never quite learned the language of the country they were living in."

"No?"

"No." She did not smile. "But *I* did. I'm grateful they didn't home-school me."

The man scowled. "Home-school you? What mean?"

"It means brainwashing your children in your own home, rather than sending them to a school – for brainwashing there." She waited for him to laugh.

But he was unsure. "You make joke?"

"It's not important. Let's continue with your form." She looked at it again.

"You have children? Yes?" the man suddenly asked.

Leona paused. "We're talking about *you*, Hamid. Is that okay?" She glanced at the form again.

Hamid looked stricken. "Oh, you don't have children. I am very sorry."

"Actually, I have two children."

"Two! Maybe even more one day?!" Hamid grinned a big grin.

"I doubt it. Two are enough." Leona shook her head slightly.

"I have three! One day three more! Everybody need many children!"

"Somehow I question that."

"My youngest child, also Hamid, is sick. Very sick. He coughs." He coughed to demonstrate.

"I'm sorry to hear that."

"Also my wife – she cough." He coughed again to demonstrate.

"Perhaps the coughs will pass. They usually do."

"Or maybe they die – my wife, my child, unless they come here? They very sick."

"I'm not sure that's the best argument for letting immigrants in, Hamid."

"No? You no like sick babies?"

"I've had my own, and if I want more I can always fly on an airplane somewhere."

"I do not follow." He shrugged.

"Back to the form! I see that you are seeking asylum from the turmoil in your home country."

"Oh, yes! Bad turmoil!"

"And what is your home country? You left that space blank."

"My country is – how you say? – 'in transition.'"

"I see. Well, we can clear that up later. There are quotas for different regions."

"Quotas?"

"Only a certain number of immigrants are permitted from different areas, given that there are so many who want to migrate." She gave him a knowing look. "But then you probably know that."

But Hamid did not nod. "What areas get most quotas?"

"It fluctuates."

"Fluctuates?"

"It changes, depending on various wars, crises, natural disasters, and so on."

"Which is it best to be from now?"

"I don't know, and I can't tell you that anyway. It might influence how you fill out the form. *Anyone*, not just you."

"Oh, no, I always tell truth! On my heart!" Hamid touched his chest. "On my baby's head! On my baby's cough!" He laughed, then looked solemn.

"I'm sure you'd do anything for your baby, Hamid. Anything."

Suddenly, Hamid fidgeted in his chair. "I'm hungry!"

"I beg your pardon?" His sudden shift had unnerved her a bit.

"I have no eating in long, long time."

"Didn't you get something to eat in the Services Department?"

"All gone! Hungry people steal bread. Even muffins. All gone when I get there."

"We're not equipped to feed people from this office. I'm sorry."

"Are hearing my stomach barking?"

"Barking?"

"You know …"

"You mean growling? Your stomach is *growling*. That is the word."

"Yes? You hear?"

"I don't. But I'm sure we can get you a snack box if necessary. Do you want a snack box? I can call for one." She reached for the phone on her desk.

"What is snack box?"

"We keep food in small boxes, for staff. And emergencies."

"*I'm* an emergency!"

"Then I'll call." She began to dial.

"What is inside this snack box?"

"Just general food: a small sandwich, cheese, a candy bar."

He looked stern. "No pork!"

"I can get you a vegetarian snack box."

"Not vegetarian. Just no pork!"

"I don't believe they put pork in any of the snack boxes, for various reasons."

"You eat pork?"

"I'm a vegan."

"So no pork. . . . Are you Jewish?"

"I don't see what that has to do with the form." She held it up.

"Jews don't eat pork, too."

"You really shouldn't ask people what religion they are. We don't do that here."

"No? Sorry!" He looked mystified. "You not proud of your religion?"

"We don't think it good to over-emphasize it. People might feel pressured. Besides, I don't practice it."

"No pressure! No pressure! No snack box!" He seemed to enjoy his word play.

"So back to your application for asylum. Shall we?"

"Yes!"

"This isn't your first time applying, true?"

"I try three times before. Fourth time the charm, yes?!"

"There are so many, many applicants."

"Let everybody come! Ha! Big party!" Such a big smile he had.

"Some people seem more interested in their personal advantage than in the general good."

"You mean you?"

"No, I mean people don't think the 'population explosion' applies to them."

"What is 'population splosion'?"

"I'm not here to lecture you. But it's clear some religions, some belief systems, whatever, over-encourage their members to have large families when … "

"Yes! Your children take care of you when you old. Don't you want your children to take care of you when you old?"

"I'll settle for a visit or two in the home." She smiled.

"The home?"

"Never mind. My children are very independent, the way we raised them."

"You and your husband?"

Leona hesitated. "Yes, me and my . . . husband."

"You married, yes? Two children!" He looked at her suspiciously.

"Again we seem to be getting off, topic, Hamid."

"Did I tell you I was attacking by mob?"

She glanced up. "What mob was that?"

"Protesters somewhere near border. They did not want us to come to that country."

"But your country was waiting with open arms for all comers, right?"

Hamid laughed. "You right! Nobody want to come to my country!"

"I don't mean to denigrate your country's suffering. It's just that . . . Well, I think I've heard enough for now. There are still numerous other migrants I must speak with. It is now mandated that each one is to receive a personal interview before … "

"Please not go yet! I not tell you of time I ate dog!"

"You ate a dog? Is that what you said?"

"I did not want to eat dog. Dogs are dirty! But I was so hungry. My family ate with me. It was an old dog."

"I'm sure the dog appreciated that you didn't eat it when it was young."

"What?"

"I'm sorry you were forced to eat a dog."

"And other disgusting things."

"We needn't list them all. I believe you."

"Even cats!"

"I believe you!"

"We find in garbage. With worms!"

Leona folded her arms. "Anything else you had to eat?"

"If you cook them, worms taste good."

"I'm sure. Maybe you'll give me your recipe."

"You not care I eat worms? My family eat worms?"

"I care, Hamid. That's why I have this job. I just can't absorb all the horrors that come my way each day."

"I miss my family!"

"I'm sure you do. Where are they now?"

"In camp. It is called the Jungle. Very crowded – my wife, our four children, her sister, my father . . ."

"I thought you said you have three children."

"Just have new baby!"

"Really?"

"No congratulations?"

". . . Congratulations."

Hamid looked her right in the eye. "You don't like me!"

"Personal favoritism plays no part in my decision. There are … "

"I think it does. Yes!"

"Are you so sure it will be better in the country you are trying to get into?"

"Not better?"

"Unemployment is very high in my country right now."

"I take any job!"

"I'm sure you will. Some people believe you will take *their* job."

"I was professional in my country."

"Oh? What kind?"

"Was legal assistant."

"Were you a lawyer?"

"No lawyer. But work for lawyer. Hard work for lawyer! I work for lawyer in your country! I very good! Very good English!"

"I'm sure. I can appreciate your argumentative skills."

"Yes? My skills?" He was excited.

"You are motivated. I can see that."

"I work like dog! Like dirty dog! Just don't eat me!" He laughed, too hard. Suddenly he said, "But forget about me. What about *you*?"

"What about *me*?" She caught herself. "No, never mind."

"You seem sad. Why you sad?"

"I'm not sad. I am trying to be professional."

"What mean 'professional'? Not care about migrants?"

"Sometimes, it may mean that, yes. I like to think one can be an empathetic – empathic? – individual. Still, there's a limit to everything."

"What about your two children? Boys?"

"No, one is a girl."

"Very nice. Girls very nice."

"Yes, I'm sure they make perfect wives, don't they?"

"Most want to be wife," Hamid said coldly.

"I'm sure the polling in your home country has been extensive on the subject."

"Polling?"

"Forget that I said that."

"You say something you shouldn't?" He looked expectantly at her.

"I'll be sure to tell you when I do."

"What about your other child – boy, girl?"

"Please, Hamid! Let's not ... "

"No, no, I want to know. I'm interest!"

"Well, as a matter of fact, I'm very proud of my son."

"Ah, a boy! Very nice." His smile couldn't have been more sincere.

"Ian is . . . transgender. We're very proud of him for choosing his own path."

"He's what?"

"Transgender."

"Pardon me, what mean 'transgender'?"

"I knew we shouldn't have veered from the topic."

"This Ian is. . . ?" He moved his hand to indicate the child might be "funny."

"That's not quite how I would put it. But we're not in any way ashamed. Ian is a lovely person."

"Yes, he sounds 'lovely.'" Hamid tried to hide his amusement. "Very, very lovely boy, I'm sure."

"You're not doing yourself any favors here. Do you realize that?"

"I'm sorry. I'm sorry. It must be lovely to have a transgender."

"Do they kill the transgender in your country?"

"No! No! . . . We do not have transgender."

"I'm sure you do. You just don't realize it."

Hamid's face fell. "I make you mad. I'm sorry! I'm sorry!"

"You haven't made me mad. In fact, I see this as a very teachable moment. Ha!" She laughed at her own pretentiousness. "Excuse me, Hamid. I have to check on something." Leona got up and left the room.

Hamid waited. He was tempted to get up from his chair and look around. But he forced himself to stay put. Impulsively, all of a sudden, he jumped up and looked at his application form, which Leona had left on the desk. Then he hurriedly started to put it back.

Leona re-entered the room carrying a snack box, and caught him at her desk. "Can I help you?" she said sharply.

"Just checking, to be sure I signed it."

"And whether *I* did?"

"No! . . . No!"

"Rest assured I won't be making a decision while you're in the room, Hamid. We find that does not make for the most objective decision. Here's a snack box if you want it." She held it out.

"Thank you, no." He did not take the snack box, and Leona put it down on her desk.

Hamid burst out with, "You like Heavy Metal?"

"Heavy Metal?"

"I fit right in. See! Also I like pizza. No anchovies! And Bing Crosby! You like Bing Crosby?" He stared at her hopefully.

"I can take him or leave him."

"How about k.d. lang?" he insinuated. "You like? With little letters?"

"What is that supposed to mean?"

"She is – how you say? – 'butch'? Is it 'butch'? 'Transgender'? She singer!"

Leona sighed. "Hamid, you're trying too hard!"

He shook his head slowly. "Cannot try too hard."

"I suppose not, when you're desperate."

"So I die in a ditch? What matter? Many more live."

"Well, Hamid, I believe I have enough information from you. Thank you for coming in." She stood.

"Oh, please, not yet over! I think you still not like me. Please, please, like me!"

"Haven't I made it clear that it's not a matter of whether I 'like' you or not?"

"Oh, it does, it does. . . . It does."

"What else do you want to discuss?" She sat back down.

"Do you want to know why my old country so full of war?"

"I have some idea. Though the reasons appear to keep changing. Old grievances, new grievances. Irreconcilable differences."

"Bad, bad people in charge! Selfish!"

"I'm sure."

"And the Jews!"

"The Jews?!"

"Bad people! . . . You're not Jewish, are you? Didn't you say?"

"I thought we covered that already. I am Jewish."

"I didn't mean . . ." His eyes darted around.

"I'm sure you didn't."

"Not all Jews!"

"Of course not."

"I'm sorry, but they are not always good!"

"It's not a matter of anybody always being good but some always being *bad*."

"If I come to your country, I will change."

"Nobody's asking you to change."

"Yes, I think so."

"And why is that?"

"From your face – I can tell."

"Well, maybe a little change wouldn't be so terrible."

"It is good for people to have different ideas, no?"

"Theoretically."

"You believe in 'diversity,' yes?" With enthusiasm: "'Diversity'!"

"The more relevant question might be: do *you* believe in 'diversity'?"

"You doubt me? I embrace 'diversity' and 'transgender' – I love!"

"Hamid!"

"And the gays! I vote for gay marriage. I promise."

"That isn't necessary."

"You not like the gays – the men?"

" . . . Not always."

"I never hurt one!"

"I could tell you were a liberal."

"You don't think I'm a liberal?"

"No."

"I am! I love all people!"

"My experience would lead me to believe you are not a liberal by the standards of my country."

"I can't seem to win." He shrugged again, harder.

"It's not a matter of winning, Hamid."

"Oh, but it is! And you are winning. I will have to go back to the Jungle, and you will go home to your . . . *husband*."

"Stop this!"

"Stop what?"

"All this . . . all this manipulation."

"I not!"

"You are, too! That's all you're doing!"

"What else am I expected to do?"

"Every other word out of your mouth is a . . . How can you expect me to trust even one syllable you say about anything?!"

"Easy to tell truth when you are comfortable, and not hungry." He hit the snack box with one hand and knocked it to the floor.

Silence.

Leona got up, retrieved the snack box, returned it to her desk, then sat again. Both said nothing.

Leona set her face. "I believe we have nothing more to say to each other."

Hamid fell to his knees. "Oh, help me! Help me, please, lady! No one will help me and my family. You have a family. Won't you be kind? You don't have to let all the migrants in. Just me!" He wept. "Just me. Just me." He collapsed to the floor, weeping harder.

Leona did not move.

Slowly, Hamid got up from the floor, embarrassed. "Sorry. I make fool. So sorry."

"I understand," she replied awkwardly. "Thank you for coming in. I mean . . ."

"I understand. You have to do what you have to do. I will leave." He wiped at his knees.

"That's probably best. I have more interviews."

"Of course. Thank you for talking to me. You are the first to spend so much time."

"We'll see what we can do, Hamid. I promise you that."

"Ha! I hear that before." He smiled ruefully. "And that makes me not hopeful."

"I have your application here."

"May I know if it is a yes or a no?"

"As I said, the decision will not be made immediately. Goodbye." She stood. She did not offer her hand.

"Okay, goodbye." He went to the exit, then turned back. "I think I know 'goodbye' when I hear it." He opened the door and left.

Leona examined the application form for a full minute, uncertain, then finally said, "Okay. Welcome, Hamid." She took a rubber stamp from a drawer in her desk and stamped his application with an approval. She then turned to another application.

Just then, Hamid re-entered the office. "I know you don't want me. I know you hate me. So I go! Bye-bye!" he spat. "How you say? – 'I'll be *back*!' And when we are many – how you say? – 'I will interview *you*!'"

He slammed the door behind him this time.

Leona waited a long time, then took Hamid's approved application form and, as she cried, began to tear it up slowly into many pieces.

[Bitter*sweet* perhaps?]

ONE HOT BABY

(This story first appeared in the anthology *Cruising*, Cleis Press, edited by Shane Allison, 2012.)

THIS IS a true story.

That doesn't make it true, of course.

It was something that happened just one time, never before and never since, and never again.

I don't mean to make it sound like a riddle. Though it was a riddle, sort of. I don't think it changed my life. Well, maybe a little.

I was on my way home from work. I'm a claims adjuster and should have retired a long time ago, but I didn't and haven't, mainly because I like my job. Oh, it's boring at times and people lie like mad trying to fool my insurance company. I suppose I enjoy catching them. I was going to be a lawyer, or so I thought, and yet somehow that never worked out. I would have been a prosecutor. You know why? Because the real problem today is not that innocent people are convicted of crimes they didn't commit. It's the crimes committed that never get punished! Where's the outcry over *that*? Just last week, there was this fellow – I won't say where he was from. Let's just say it wasn't from America – who was trying to screw the hell out of my company by claiming that his grandmother was entitled to money from the accident he was in because – get this! – he was unable to move her to the States the way he'd been planning to because now she said Americans were dangerous drivers and she was afraid to come after his accident, an accident which he caused!

But don't get me started.

I was on my way home and needed to take a leak so bad I could taste it. It had been a very bad day. My boss, who is thirty-six – I'm seventy-two – chewed me out for not filling out some form properly, something I've done for fifty-one years. The worst part is that he was right. I think my memory is going a bit. I really should retire, but what am I going to do, sit around and twiddle my fingers? My retired friend Frank complains all the time that he is bored out of his mind. He has taken up baby-sitting some feral cats behind his house and going to a shabby mall twice a day just to have something to do.

Anyway, it was not a good day – it was yesterday I'm talking about. I got a haircut at the barbershop next door to my office during my lunch break, and as I sat in the barber's chair with all this awful hair from other customers littering the floor – Gus won't sweep it up except once a day, claims he's too busy even though I tell him it looks awful – I looked, really *looked,* at my reflection in the mirrors. Gus has several of them on both sides of his shop, so there's no escaping what you look like. And I noticed that I'm really starting to age. I've always looked younger than I am, by a good ten years. Only yesterday I could see a bald patch in the back that I usually can't see in the mirror in my bathroom. Well, here it was, with all this gray hair around it, some of it sticking up on the left side even though I had wetted it down that morning. It made me look like a jerk. Next to my right eye I could see an age spot coming through, and they're coming through on the backs of my hands, too. It's Death rotting you from the inside out. There were also pouches under my eyes, not huge ones, but I never used to have pouches! The skin on my face looked loose. This is what I get for losing thirty pounds by eating goddamned low-calorie bread sticks and steamed cauliflower for the last six months! The hair grows in my ears, too, and now it's not only too long, it's gray.

So I'm sitting there looking at myself, and Gus, who's pallid and Greek and ninety if he's a day, says to me, "You been sick, Artie?"

I didn't answer him. And I didn't give him a tip, either. He gives lousy haircuts, always has. I don't know why I keep going there.

"You look hunched over," Gus goes on as if I'm there for a beauty consultation. This from a guy who practically invented osteoporosis himself. "You need some calcium, Artie," he tells me.

"Yeah, yeah," I said. "Why don't you clean up the fucking hair off the floor?"

He didn't talk to me after that. Which left no small talk, and I had to sit there and stare at my seventy-two-year-old face. Sure, it's natural to age. Nature sucks.

Anyhoo, I'm driving home to take a leak like there's no tomorrow and I drive by this park. I've driven by it a thousand times before. I never go there. Let's face it, I'm not a hiker, barely a walker.

It's getting dark because it's close to winter, and there's no restroom in the park, I'm pretty sure, because they closed it, I read. So I parked my car to relieve myself of the two diet Pepsis I'd had to keep on my diet, and I went up this little path with all these cypress trees alongside it, some vegetation. Don't ask me to name it. I'm terrible at flowers and stuff like that. It was pretty dense because we've had a lot of rain.

I thought I wasn't going to make it and might actually pee in my pants. You probably don't want to hear about it, but that's happened to me a few times recently. Just couldn't hold it. The old prostate is kicking the bucket, my doctor says. Not cancer, thank god, just ENLARGED. Well, at least something got enlarged with time! Somehow, I managed to whip the old wiener out despite the goddamn pinching zipper and the fucking underwear. There I am standing, spewing like the god of urine, whoever that is, and feeling so lucky to be a guy and not have to squat to piss. I must have uncorked a quart, if it was an ounce. "Thank you, God!" I said under my breath. I say that every time I have a good pee these days. The stupid Flomax isn't all it's cracked up to be. And I forget to take it sometimes, I have to admit.

So I'm putting away the old equipment and I notice this young guy standing there halfway behind a tree. He's about thirty, slender, with a little mustache. I think his hair was dark brown. I know it was short. He was wearing just regular clothes — pants, jacket, I couldn't even say what color they were. Gray, the jacket was gray. Oh, and he was wearing a black-and-orange baseball cap. Whatever. I notice that he's half-looking at my dick, or at least the crotch. Well, guys just don't do that, I'm here to tell you! I started to say something to him, but he turned away. So I turned away, too, having some more trouble with that zipper, while heading back to my car.

And then, for some reason, I stopped. I could lie and say it was to enjoy the night air, but actually it was getting more than a little cold. I could say I stopped to smell the roses, but those flowers around me out there weren't roses. I know that much.

Then suddenly, this guy was back in sight. He looked right into my eyes. I didn't look away. We both waited to see what was what. I thought I knew what he might be there for, but I didn't know for sure. I mean, he wasn't queeny or anything, and he didn't point to his butt. Isn't that what they do? How would I know? He was very cautious and took his time. I just sort of stood there with my fingers on my zipper. I felt sort of silly, to be honest, and I almost left.

But I didn't. After a while, the guy sauntered over and checked me out. It was getting dark and I suppose the bad light did me a good turn. He was most interested in my crotch, but he did look right into my face, too. And he didn't turn and run, the way I thought he would. In fact, he got down on his knees, slowly, turned his cap around, and began sucking my wiener like he was no vegetarian, let me tell you! I filled up his mouth, and I didn't even need my Viagra. I watched his head going back and forth. He was really into it. It did not last very long, but it didn't have to at that rate.

"Thank you, God!" I called out as I was coming, not too loud, just a little bit, and he took it all, every drop, every seventy-two-year-old drop in me. And when he got up from his knees and looked me in the face again, he smiled and said the nicest words I probably have ever heard in my whole life:

"You're one hot baby." And, no, he wasn't being sarcastic, asshole! He meant it.

Was it the greatest day of my life? . . . No. Was it the greatest day of the past five years and probably the next five years? . . . Probably.

And then he went his way, and I went mine, like ships in the night. The cocksucker and One Hot Baby. Thank you, God.

I don't think I'll tell my wife this story.

THE CAMPY SACRED HEART OF JESUS

MY "WICKED" PAST is catching up with me. I recently found a Sacred Heart of Jesus ceramic art piece in a box behind some old stored books in my basement. I was cleaning up after my partner's death at the age of sixty-nine. We were together for thirty-seven years, minus a month or two (or three) when we were quarreling. His big old body is awaiting cremation at a crematorium as I write this. He has been there for two weeks, frozen, because there's been a delay.

The Sacred Heart of Jesus that I found was given to me by an old trick named Ron Something.

I had quite a little crush on him at the time. I don't favor redheads usually, but his was dark red and the accompanying freckles impish and under control. He was thinner than I like and not that well hung, but he knew how to hold your interest when he talked and knew a lot about art because he had studied it in college and was making these ceramic Sacred Hearts of Jesus, beautiful and serious, but at the same time campy: a Sacred Heart of Jesus with barbecue sauce for blood, a Sacred Heart of Jesus with chocolate sprinkles. The one he gave me had a baby Jesus clinging to its side, hanging on for dear life. I took it out of the box to examine it for any damage. It seemed in pretty good shape. I was amazed because it had been there for over thirty years. There wasn't even any water damage.

I had encouraged Ron Something to finish the set of Sacred Hearts and get them into a gallery or even a museum. He demurred, saying, "They won't sell. They're too campy for the truly religious and too religious for the truly campy." I thought they were terrific.

And then Ron Something moved away to Southern California and took his wonderful self and art with him. We had a couple of phone calls, but his partner got jealous, and so the calls stopped. You know how those things go. Oh, my own partner and I always had an open relationship. I had violated it by getting *emotionally* involved with somebody else, instead of just sex. "How's your boyfriend?" my partner, Max, would tease me from time to time, touching his heart to mock me. "Are you moving to Southern California? Hmm?"

"I'll send you a postcard when I get there," I'd tease back. Have you noticed how much "teasing" is nasty when you look at it?

I thought maybe Ron Something and I would perhaps meet up down the road and reminisce about old times, even the one semi-disastrous time we attempted actual sex. But instead I got word that Ron had died. It wasn't AIDS. It certainly wasn't old age. He was thirty-two and just fell asleep by his fireplace and didn't wake up. It could have been carbon monoxide. It could have been drugs. It could have been a faulty heart. Maybe it was a punishment from God for those campy Sacred Hearts of Jesus? (I doubt it. They were lovely and God knew it. Maybe God was jealous.)

At the time, I wept a bit for Ron Something and his lost potential. He was talented and yet lacked drive. I don't know what happened to the other Sacred Hearts of Jesus. Maybe the boyfriend had them? Maybe they were all crushed in an earthquake? The world is, I've heard, not very kind to art, especially delicate ceramics.

On a lark, I took the Sacred Heart I'd found to a fine art dealer I'd seen on TV. I thought maybe he could place it somewhere. I hated the idea of it just sitting in a box or being thrown into a dump truck when I die. I suppose that is what will happen to all the "things" I've saved over the years. To my surprise, the art dealer loved the campy Sacred Heart. He said that because there was a baby on it, it would probably sell "in a heartbeat." He offered me ten thousand dollars for it. I'm sure he later sold it for at least double, but I was thrilled that it would be valued by somebody. He said that if it had been created by somebody who had died of AIDS it would be worth even more. I couldn't authenticate that, however. I accepted his offer and used the money to pay some bills, including the one for my partner's cremation. I hadn't had enough in the bank to pay for it. But thanks to the gift from that old trick I'd had a crush on for a time, I was able to pay the crematorium and have big Max's little ashes finally placed in our reserved burial space there.

As I stood in front of it, I whispered to him, "Hold on, honey. I'm coming. It won't be long."

IT'S NOT EASY BEING GOD

DEVON LAPUKE (pronounced La Pook) was a struggling forty-five-year-old would-be novelist who was writing what he thought to be the Great American Novel. It had already been written, in fact several times, but LaPuke did not appear to be aware of this. You see, he rarely read anything himself, so obsessed with his own book was he. He was also so devoted to his novel that he barely ate and thus kept his naturally heavyset body both thin and wiry and his black eyes fiery, making him very attractive, to some. He was a driver for Lyft, a job that allowed him plenty of time to write. He had sent out the thirty pages of his novel to several literary agents and editors, but none had been willing to take on the book. LaPuke was growing desperate.

Then one of his Lyft fares turned out to be an actress (not that well known), and yet it crossed his mind that perhaps she might want to make a movie out of his book. He began flirting with the actress, not at all subtly, knowing that his wiry appeal often worked on the ladies, and he had eight thick inches to back him up whenever he wanted them. She was hardly hard to flirt with, very pretty with far too much makeup on and those spindly little arms, as the fashion would have it. She flirted back as the meter ticked away.

"Would you like to hear some of the Great American Novel?" he pressed.

"I suppose," replied the pretty actress, somewhat taken aback.

"I can recite some of it from memory," LaPuke said.

"Have you seen my movie?" she asked.

"I'm afraid I haven't."

"Okay, I'll listen to your novel, if you promise to go see my movie."

"It's a deal," he said. "The title of my book is *It's Not Easy Being God*."

"Sounds good," she said.

So with his hands on the wheel and his eyes on the road – and occasionally on the pretty actress – LaPuke began his tale. "Now that I have, somewhat miraculously, been given the powers of a shape-shifter plus the ability to use any method I wish in order to change the world, I have decided to lay out on these pages my actions and thoughts for all to follow, a Bible no doubt to marvel at. To kill or not to kill, to maim, hinder, alter, help, or to leave alone – those are the questions that consume me as I embark on this momentous, possibly dark, journey to improve the world. Follow me if you care to, but I answer to no one but myself."

The actress didn't especially like the tone and moved uncomfortably on the passenger seat.

LaPuke hurried on. "There is a man I have come to loathe with a loathing that exceeds rationality. I may have liked him once, but now he torments my every day, with his incessant misstating of figures, never mind false predictions, which he never apologizes for. I speak, of course, of Bill Martin, a weatherman on television. His long, unpleasant body and horse teeth and pale skin only serve to encapsulate his dreary and repetitive "forecasts," and so I have decided to eliminate Bill Martin from the universe. I suppose I could simply just not watch him on TV anymore, but I would know that he still is broadcasting his awfulness to others, others who lack my special powers. I believe it is my duty to remove him from this world because he apparently will never retire from his job as a meteorologist. This afternoon, through sheer mental exertion, I sent out a drone equipped with a brick to drop on his head when he arrived at work at his TV station. I had estimated his time of arrival from hints during his broadcasts in the past. Alas, when released, the drone brick missed him. Instead, it hit an elderly Asian lady in a Lark (a motorized scooter) as she raced for a bus and knocked her senseless, according to the hysterical news report at ten o'clock. It even led to speculation by the News Team that they might be the targets of a deranged killer. No, only Bill Martin, the weatherman, is the target. I will try again tomorrow. He is known to body surf the ocean on Wednesdays. I may take advantage of his hobby and send a mechanical shark to pull him under to his death. It can't come soon enough.

"With my special powers, I am sending out a *real* shark to get Bill Martin, the weatherman, this afternoon. I have examined the shark's details on the view screen in my head and configured the sharpest teeth and the biggest mouth on a Great White that I can muster. I have noticed that one can add too many apps and gadgets and buttons to anything and wind up with a nonfunctioning piece of crap. This shark is going to work on that fatuous weatherman or my name isn't the Great Corrector!"

"How do you like it so far?" LaPuke asked the actress.

"It's different," she replied. "Is Bill Martin a local weathercaster? I don't believe I've seen him."

"This just in!" LaPuke continued. "The shark I sent did attack Bill Martin at a beach on the ocean. It ripped off both his arms, according to the ten o'clock news. He bled prodigiously and the blood attracted other sharks that I didn't even send. At first, they thought the man would not survive such an attack. Yet he managed to drag himself through the surf onto the beach. There, several seagulls pecked at his eyes, and, having no arms, he could not defend himself. Eventually, some paramedics arrived and gave Bill Martin first aid. They were thus able to save his life. On the matter of his forecasting, he was forced to retire since he no longer had either arms or eyes and could not see or point to the temperatures on the TV weather map. He was replaced as meteorologist by a small female of Pakistani descent, who was better, and I decided to let her live, at least for a while."

"I think that's my stop up there," said the actress, trying to open the door.

"Can I have your card?" LaPuke said. "Here's mine." He fished one out of the glove compartment.

"And mine," she said. She thrust it into his hand.

It wasn't until she was out of his car and running off that he noticed that her card had neither address nor telephone number on it. He went to see her movie, and it was bad, and she was bad in it. He hoped that she wouldn't call him, and she didn't.

About a week later, LaPuke picked up another fare in his car. It was a gay man, very fat. He could barely get into the back seat. He was wearing just a white T-shirt and shorts, even though it was cold out. "I've been working out," the fare said. "Do you work out?"

One thing led to another, and soon LaPuke was reciting his novel to the fat gay man, but they were not in LaPuke's car. The fare had insisted that the recitation take place in his apartment, specifically on his couch with LaPuke, still clothed, pressing his eight thick inches into the pelvic area of the fat gay man, also still clothed. It was understood that no penetration of any kind was going to take place. Since LaPuke was one hundred and ten percent heterosexual, he found his pelvic position rather awkward, and he feared that his breath might be bad, but his fat gay fare didn't seem to mind and awaited the recitation.

LaPuke decided he would read a different section for the fat gay man than he had for the pretty actress. He began. "In any given time period, there are prevailing waves of thought, if what makes people act even rises to the level of thought much of the time. In my time, you cannot say anything critical of 'people of color' without being called a racist. People have allowed the prevailing

148

wave of thought on this topic, at least publicly, to go all one way. They are terrified of the word 'racist.' Their voices tremble when 'race' is mentioned. Having a Discussion About Race means a bunch of black people yelling at 'people of non-color' and telling them they are the whole problem and nothing but."

Even though he seemed to be enjoying the thick eight inches of LaPuke's "equipment" pressed into his fully clothed pelvic area, the fat gay man stirred and said, "Do you have any other section of your book that you might recite to me? Something *not* about race?"

LaPuke had anticipated as much and quickly searched his mind. "It does not take much historical oversight to see that most wars, whatever their causes, use young men to fight them. Sometimes the reasons for the wars make a little sense, but often these wars just seem idiotic when viewed objectively. The young male soldiers usually are horny and bored, and will do anything to get a fuck and some adventure."

LaPuke could feel the fat gay fare get hard, still clothed.

"Therefore, today I began setting up Sex and Violence Booths on several street corners in the vicinity of my lair. I thought about putting them on public sidewalks; however, the police very likely would demolish them immediately. I could demolish the interfering police, true, but they tend to be unrelenting in going after anyone who hurts their own, and I want this program to at least get off the ground. So I put the Sex and Violence Booths on private vacant lots instead. I am convinced that few men will run off to fight wars in far-flung places if they can get their rocks off near where they live.

"The desire to be someplace – any place – *else* is universal. So I have installed, via my special powers, Booths that not only satisfy any reasonable person's sex drive, but provide 3D virtual tours of exotic locales, such as Iraq, Afghanistan, Central America, Tibet, Qatar, and even Toledo, Ohio (the latter being exotic if you are from any other place on earth). The virtual tours as they are broadcast in the darkened environment will make the customer feel as if he is in the Alps, on a tiger hunt in India, on a beach in Tahiti, captured by indigenous Communists in the Philippines, or anywhere else the DJ in charge can program. In a separate wing, young men can play video games before or after they fuck. They can even get hit by shrapnel, bayonets, or anything else they choose, getting large wounds or small, according to taste, and come away with war scars they can display with pride once treated and released by the medical staff. Distinguished service medals can be purchased separately.

"Here is how the Sex Booths themselves will work: The horny young male pays what he wishes, from five dollars to nothing, as an entrance fee, on a sliding scale, depending on whether he likes free sex or having to pay for it. Attendants will then show the customer to a series of short corridors. At the end of each is a Hole of Glory where various body parts will be on display for the customers' use. These include female genitalia (probably the most popular orifice), thighs (male or female), mouths (male, female, or undetermined), anuses (clean, dirty, or to be determined as used, for those who like surprises). I am not sure if a nose or an ear would appeal to enough customers to maintain staff in that arena of sexual proclivity. I, of course, will be paying for personnel to provide these genitalia, thighs, mouths, and anuses that serve our clientele. I have endless money to use and am committed to full employment; still, it doesn't hurt to be frugal, to protect against a rainy day. The customer in each Sex Booth will be offered a choice of body part, or even several. Full-blown orgies will no doubt join the list of services once the kinks are worked out. Delayed gratification in an orgy setting will likely contribute to ongoing interest in the Booths. A customer who prefers to pursue a desired sexual object rather than have it merely thrust into his face can signal his desire by pushing a button, and the thighs, genitalia, mouths, and/or anuses will play hard to get. Some may even contain teeth or sandpaper to keep the game exciting. What about those who want to have their sex lying down in a bed? Or who want to see an entire body while engaged in sex or to cuddle with before or afterwards? Nobody gets everything he wants even in this Utopia!

"To ensure protection against venereal diseases, the customer will be required to use proper protection, whether that be a condom or any current or new antiviral medications. Needless to say, going from one body part to another, while not advised, is permitted if the customer changes any soiled protection between 'engagements' in the Holes of Glory. Yes, it may be a nuisance, but the customer has to play his part.

"The hard-working Sex Workers will be checked hourly by a team of doctors to guard against diseases and damage. They will, of course, be unionized and remunerated for their service to their country. People in general will be rewarded with redeemable coupons for exciting gifts if they recognize a Holes of Glory Sex Worker in the outside world and say, 'Thank you for your service. God bless America!' Or China! Bolivia! Etc., etc.

"Is it possible that some horny men will turn down these proffered delights? Possibly, I suppose. Perhaps one of the Booths provided can say, 'Love Here,' and the customer can whisper sweet nothings or listen to such while ejaculating or playing with a preferred body part. Who am I to judge? There might even be other sex acts that do not quite fit under the grand plan laid out here. I am sure that, with feedback from customers and some fine-tuning about fetishes, we can eventually satisfy every horny young male in the world with Sex Booths in every nation, on every corner, in all the known languages, including Sign, and end war as we know it."

The fat gay man that LaPuke was lying on top of seemed to be enjoying the novel. And so he went on:

"Now, someone has asked about females and their sex needs. There naturally will be Sex Booths available for women. Something tells me they will not be used much. This may distress those devoted to Equal Rights in all areas of human behavior. But I don't think very many women run off to war to get fucked. If they do, they don't need my Sex Booths. They can go sign up with ISIS. And what about the customers who want sex with children or animals? Why would they need my Sex Booths? I'm not asking for families to change their practices. And are the farmyards closed?! The only real problem I see with my plan is that the marriage rate will decline, there being little need for it now. The burgeoning human population explosion will be curtailed, finally. Those wishing to have offspring can apply for a special permit and make their own arrangements. Yes, these people may further the cause of perpetual warfare, because of their need to replicate themselves, to protect their property, but when offered cheap Sex Booths versus the rigors of family life as the price for sex, I think I know who will win most of the time, especially if people from kindergarten on are shown videos of *actual* family life instead of the usual lies."

"You're quite cynical about sex," said the fat gay man, removing himself from the couch.

"Am I?"

"I'd like you to leave."

So LaPuke left the man's apartment.

Three days later, another interesting fare got into his car. Thirteen others that day had refused to listen to any of LaPuke's Great American Novel, but this gentleman was encouraging. He looked to be Iranian, of patrician carriage, most likely an expatriate because of the Fundamentalist Revolution. He was carrying several books, on classical music, mathematics, mechanical engineering, and world literature. He wore crisp casual clothes and was in his mid-forties, and had a furrowed brow.

LaPuke took the risk of reciting all of what he had written for *It's Not Easy Being God*, since the gentleman said he loved audible books and the ride to his destination was long. Here is the part you didn't hear before:

"I had to use my shape-shifting power today for the first time. It went pretty well, though not perfectly. It turns out that there are wild coyotes in my neighborhood. I live in a large metropolitan city, I point out. You would think coyotes would have been a problem solved in the distant past. But no, some half dozen have come back. One of my dogs, a French pug, was almost killed today by a coyote attack. I was carrying Mr. Puggles in my arms after our walky-poo in a nearby park since Mr. Puggles is thirteen and has elbow issues. Not one but two coyotes stalked me and Mr. Puggles with their cruel, cold eyes and then leapt from two directions at once and dragged Mr. Puggles from my arms, even though I had crossed them over his body. They proceeded to eat one of his legs as blood spurted everywhere. My other French pug, Ms. Waffles, barked at the mayhem that was going on, but she did not go after the coyotes. Truth be told, Ms. Waffles is fourteen, not too bright, and a pacifist. In all, there were five coyotes, three making a semi-circle in front of me, two eating Mr. Puggles's leg. Several other dog walkers attempted to help, but they were ineffectual against the barbaric hunger of the coyotes. One woman, in fact, looked smug and said, 'That's what you get for not keeping your dogs on a leash!' I replied, 'I think I have earned the right to walk my sweet little, harmless dogs any way I want to.' And the lady said, 'Coyotes are a native species, and they have every right to be here, even more than your imperialist French pugs!' I was speechless for a moment, then said, 'I can't wait for saber-toothed tigers to be re-introduced to the neighborhood!' The lady sniffed and hurried off with her leashed dachshund-chihuahua mix.

"Having no more time for ironic wordplay, I decided to use my shape-shifter power and willed myself into a gray wolf. I went after the closest coyote, the one holding Mr. Puggles's poor dangling front leg, and snapped my jaws around its muzzle. I loved the feel of my fangs penetrating that coyote's flesh. I thanked myself that I had made me bigger and even more ruthless than the *coyotl* of Aztec days. Yes, another coyote tore into my left haunch, causing me to yelp like a goddamned beta for a few seconds. But then I recovered and turned and slashed at the second coyote. He went racing off to a nearby stand of trees, howling like the loser he was. 'Oh, no! You're not eating Mr. Puggles!' I shouted, turning back to the first coyote. Alas, he was already eating Mr. Puggles's leg, having ripped it free from my poor dog's body. Somehow, despite my terror and pity, I bit out an eye of the first coyote and picked up the severed dog leg in my lathering mouth and put Ms. Waffles on my back, and we three raced to a veterinarian office, where I resumed human shape and they were able to reattach Mr. Puggles's front leg. I realize now that I could have used my all-encompassing special powers, which include veterinarian skills, but in the melee I forgot. Mr. Puggles walks with a decided limp now, and he stays around me on the couch even more than before, but we showed those coyotes and native-species holier-than-thou's a thing or two about who is going to dominate in this dog-eat-dog world!"

"How is it so far?" LaPuke asked the Iranian exile with the furrowed brow and the books.

"Let me hear some more before I say anything."

It didn't take being asked twice for LaPuke to respond. "Today a so-called homeless man was sitting on a bench in a downtown area as I walked by minding my own business, i.e., improving the world, and suddenly he began shouting obscenities at me. None of them were original, so I need not repeat them. There was nothing original about this homeless man, either: unwashed cheeks and forehead, scraggly, whitish beard, chapped lips, bloodshot eyes, stinking clothes, alcoholic breath.

"I veered from my path to avoid the avalanche of obscenities, but he stood up and blocked my path. I said, 'Excuse me.' And he said, 'Leave me alone!' Since I was trying to leave him alone, I did not appreciate the sagacity of his apprehension. It began to dawn on me that I have been much too nice so far in my efforts to improve the world. What this homeless man represented in the grand scheme of things except a Bad Example, it was difficult to see. 'Are you going to stop blocking my path?' I asked, moving to his right. 'Make me!' the homeless man said. It should be noted that the term 'homeless' is hopelessly misapplied. He was a drunk, a derelict, possibly also on drugs with a *soupçon* of mental illness thrown in, belligerent, confrontational, drenched in his own feces and urine (and possibly other people's as well), and standing with arms akimbo to prevent my moving anywhere but backwards. No doubt the poor fellow had had misfortunes galore, plus faulty DNA, and even lots of bad luck, but *this* bleeding heart bled out ages ago, and so I decided to act instead of put up with his shit (literally and figuratively) any longer. First, I used my special power of teleportation and sent the homeless man to a homeless shelter a few blocks away. He was back in front of me before I could take a step. 'I don't like it there!' he said to me. 'They won't let me steal!' I scratched my head and used another special power. This time, I teleported the stinky one to a SRO (single room occupancy) in a nearby old hotel, examining it to make sure it had a clean bed, a bathroom, a refrigerator, and a supply of groceries. Mr. Homeless was back in front of me by the time I had taken one step on my way to my destination. 'What's wrong with it?' I asked. 'Too small!' he snapped. 'Well, it's the same size as my apartment,' I countered. 'I like the drama of the streets!' Mr. Homeless informed me. We argued for several more minutes – in fact, it was almost an hour – and he made his case for living on the street and showed me how to dispose of feces in a Starbucks cup and to piss at the curbside. He made very good points, but eventually I decided that he was too full of shit and I simply vaporized him. It didn't hurt, I'm pretty sure. If it did, at least it didn't last as long as dying on the streets would have. And then I went on my way. 'One!' I cried out, like the vengeful Count of Monte Cristo."

LaPuke turned his head to the Iranian in the back seat. "Well?"

"Harsh about the poor," he replied.

"I have never understood why we're supposed to feel extra sympathy for the poor, that is, even more sympathy than we might feel for anybody who has to be a human being. I have found them to be obnoxious and unsightly, often. Somebody once said, the poor are something we will always have with us. If that's true, then why waste time feeling so sorry for what seems inevitable? They certainly shouldn't be encouraged to replicate themselves. People seem to care very little for anything except themselves. Give me, give me, give me! The world is choking with people, and yet, as soon as they can, they have offspring. Terrible diseases from insects, viruses, bacteria, and religious beliefs continue to cripple and destroy human populations. Then, as soon as a cure is invented, they are at it again, swelling their ranks to unsustainable levels, polluting the waters with their waste, over-spilling borders, competing for jobs, housing, and breathing space. No, the poor do not seem to learn much and are not a lot of fun. I'm not saying this because I am rich. I'm not. The rich aren't special, either. They don't usually panhandle you for a dollar, but they can be obnoxious with their Mercedes Benzes, VIP seating, and staff. If I had to choose between saving a poor person and a rich person, I would find it hard to decide. The rich person might give me a reward, although I have noticed the rich can be quite stingy. A poor person might give me a hug. But the hug might be accompanied by cooties. Perhaps it is best not to try to save any of them, just let Nature take its course. And it will. Oh, it will. I can hear you asking, 'Who appointed *you* God?!' And you're absolutely right. But I *am* God now, and I have to live with it. You can't be wishy-washy and still be God."

"I disagree with you," said the Iranian in the back seat. "But it is an interesting point of view."

"I have more," LaPuke said.

"Proceed with your novel."

"I am wondering if an Eat the Homeless Food Program might do any good. Where I happen to live, the homeless are everywhere, and it's not even a depression. They have set up tents under overpasses to guard against rain; they have spread to many public streets and public parks; their needles from their drug use decorate the landscape. It is true that some of the homeless kill themselves with overdoses and unsanitary habits, but they seem to replace themselves in no time. I did not mind them for many years, but this morning, my French pug, Mr. Puggles, stepped on a pile of human shit and a used hypodermic needle on our walk, and that was inside the walled compound that we call home. So it is past time to end the homeless problem. Many, many solutions have been proffered, all to little avail.

"One new thought is to offer Homeless Stew at the various Christian feeding stations currently in operation. Or possibly call it Diversity Stew and include dark, white, and brown meats mixed with some hearty vegetables and rice, with a gluten-free dessert. People donate their eyes, kidneys, hearts, and such to accident victims now. Why not donate one's body to the Eat the Homeless program? The resulting meat might require a thorough decontamination processing, or indeed several, to rid the food of impurities of various kinds, but it would go a long way to providing nutrition for many who might go hungry otherwise. Let me hasten to add that the Eat the Homeless program would not be just for the snooty, high-income folk, who are so often condemned for their heartlessness, but would be especially aimed at the homeless, who I'm sure can find it a step up from rummaging in garbage bins for thrown-away foodstuffs. They are also known to be mean to each other anyway.

"It might be preferable to make donating one's body voluntary, all things considered, but other options might have to be employed if volunteers fail to step up to the 'plate,' so to speak. Yes, cannibalism has gotten a bad reputation over time. But it is merely a matter of making one's body serve a higher need. It works in cultures where martyrdom for religious purposes is prized. There is no reason eating the homeless can't be made into a sacred duty, good for eaters and eaten both."

The Iranian gentleman in the back seat stroked his chin. "I assume you are alluding to 'A Modest Proposal', the satire by Jonathan Swift, not giving your true opinion."

"Who?" said LaPuke.

"Maybe just a bit more," said the Iranian gentleman. "Do you have anything that's entertaining, not just railing?"

LaPuke realized that maybe he should ease up a bit. Even in his novel, he had realized this:

"It has become obvious to me that I have a lot of dislikes. Lest I become monotonous on this topic, I have looked about for something positive to help with. I think I have found it in the Right to Pee Movement in Mumbai, India. Evidently, the public toilets there are primarily for men. Women have to pee at home or else hold it in. I am torn as to whether I should send thousands of public potties to that benighted area or do something else. These public potties will have to be cleaned constantly, or at least occasionally, to maintain sanitation, creating new jobs for that overpopulated nation but possibly spreading the stench of urine even further in that Not-Fair City. What if I use my special powers to rid the poor women of the need to pee at all? Or even to defecate? Who thought of such an arrangement for the human body in the first place?! I cannot believe in a God who invented excretion. I don't know what will happen to the food consumed by the millions whose elimination I eliminate. I might have to make it dissolve into nothingness. Or should I go even further and eliminate the need to eat and drink altogether? I guess I will take it one step at a time. So, for now, I am mustering my powers and stopping all peeing by all women in Mumbai. We'll see how that goes."

"Have you nothing sweet to say?" begged the Iranian in the back seat.

"Let me see!" said LaPuke.

He remembered something:

"As I write here today in what I see now is God's diary I sat outside in my small garden, feeling the need for some warmth and fresh air. Sometimes I think I watch too much television. I have let my Facebook account lapse; still, the world wants to impose itself and all its woes upon my brain. I have learned that just sitting in my small garden can take away the worst of it. Amazing how different the world seems when you don't allow it to step on your face every minute of the day. As I sat under a large plant with trumpet flowers – I don't know its name – I noticed two butterflies flitting about. I think they were monarchs, black and orange. I believe I read somewhere that butterflies rarely live very long, only eight months under ideal conditions, usually much less. Even the butterflies that migrate aren't the same ones who start out on their long flights. They're the grandchildren! They require a very narrow food source, like milkweed plants, and they could die out as a species if food and resting and hatching environments are not preserved.

"My personal butterflies did not really seem to be aware of me; instead, they chased each other and soared and dipped among the trumpets of my tree. I don't have any milkweed in my garden, I'm pretty sure, but the butterflies didn't seem to mind. I saw no birds pursuing them. Lizards? Who eats butterflies? I did see the Siamese cat from the next garden over eyeing my butterflies with its cold, efficient eyes. 'Don't you dare!' I gritted at the cat, who blinked a few times and licked its front leg, still plotting against the butterflies. I saw something stir near the back wall and realized it was something mammalian and white. I held my breath and my posture in my plastic chair as it moved from behind a large stone medallion I had placed against the back wall. It was a possum, with white fur and red-tinged eyes. It did not appear to see me. It did move its head when one of the two monarchs fluttered near it. Do possums eat butterflies? I wondered. Is there much nutrition in a butterfly? But the possum made no moves toward the butterflies. I tried to remain very quiet, but my plastic chair creaked, and the possum saw me. It panicked a bit and started to scurry back and forth. A neighbor had put up extra slats on his side of the fence, to keep my dogs from going through to his yard, most likely. So the possum couldn't get through the fence and escape. It started to make a sound of distress. 'It's okay. It's okay!' I said, keeping my voice soft. But the possum didn't believe me and scuttled off through the other fence on the other side of my garden. The two butterflies also thought better of my presence and ascended up into the sky and then disappeared from my sight. They had all made me happy for a few minutes, and I blessed them with a wave of my hand. Then I dozed for a bit, and when I awoke, some fog had rolled in and I, chilled but happy, free of possums and butterflies, went three blocks over to order some take-out food.

"As I waited for my pot stickers, Mongolian beef, and shrimp egg foo yung in the cramped little place, the Chinese proprietor in her thick bifocals and dirty apron kept leaning over to ring up payments on her credit card machine. There was a stool between where she wrote up the orders and where she slid the credit cards. Surely, her back must hurt from the long reach, a meter at least. I smiled and said, 'You should move the stool. Less space.' I demonstrated by pushing my hands together. The owner gave me a suspicious look and wiped a sweaty lock of hair out of her eyes. I don't think she understood English very well or else figured I was up to something. 'Move the stool. Save your back,' I said. But she went on stretching her body needlessly. Life is hard enough without making it even harder by being so stubborn, is it not? As I left with my order, I put an extra hundred-dollar bill on the counter, saying 'May I?' and took the stool with me when she nodded. See, God is watching over his flock.

"The Chinese woman muttered under her breath, 'Die, racist-round eye pig!'

"I did not smite her and let her off with a smile and a harmless wave of my hand."

***

"Well?" LaPuke inquired.

"I'd like to publish it," the gentleman replied.

"You would?" LaPuke's heart soared.

"I'd like to bring it out next year. Can you get the manuscript to me at my office?"

"You're a publisher?!" LaPuke exulted. "Oh, my God, I have a publisher. And the Great American Novel will be published at last!"

The publisher held up his forefinger as a caution. "Oh, the manuscript is too long and much, much too bitter. We will certainly have to trim it way back."

LaPuke was thrown for a loop – but only for a few moments. "Yes, yes, yes, and we'll call it the *Great American Short Story* now, okay?"

"I love it!" shouted the publisher with a heart of gold. "And I'm sure your other books will be better!"

[Are you sucking up to somebody here?]

[Of course not. Never!]

THE GRUDGE

DAN HASN'T SEEN Joyce in forty-seven years, not since he asked her for a favor in London and she had refused, had said he had "destroyed" their friendship. The details are getting fuzzy now, with the passage of time, but he remembers the hurt as if it were yesterday.

At the time, he had published a gay novel, not just any gay novel, but the very first gay protest novel, back when it was courageous and dangerous. It had come out from a major press, but it had sold only eighteen hundred copies, disappointing the publisher and impoverishing Dan, who had counted on book sales to keep him, an American, in London with some form of income. Tired of grading essays for a university that catered to U.S. airmen, he had stopped asking for courses to teach and was hoping against hope, now that he was a WRITER at last, that he would be able to make a living that way. He was wrong and he was running out of money.

Then his old friend, Joyce, wrote to say that she and her husband, Ray, were coming to London for a year, during her sabbatical from Princeton. She said how much she wanted to see him again, to go out to lunches with him as they had in Detroit, when Detroit was still livable. She hoped that the two of them would be able to renew their friendship. He hoped so, too. He had always liked Joyce, had liked her before she had become world-famous, liked her even when she was moody and slightly hysterical. He was lonely in London, working on another novel, a funny one, not so grim, artistically fulfilled, but craving companionship. His housemate was off in Iceland teaching those same airmen. There they would be, Joyce and Dan, two famous writers spending time together, the stuff of literary legend. Or so he hoped.

Only Joyce had spoiled it all by ending their friendship because he had written her a note soon after her arrival in London. He hadn't dared ask her in person. He knew that she was prickly, quick to take offense, and always just on the edge of sanity. Luckily, most of her instability came out in her numerous works of fiction and only occasionally in real life. He recalled that awkward time he had called her attention to the fact that she always misused the word "itch," confusing it with "scratch." She blew up and didn't speak to him for a month.

In general, he always had to watch his every word, to cover his tracks, to pretend to be interested in the parade of women that Joyce, only half-jokingly, said he ought to marry. She was always teasing him about not being married. She thought every man should be married. He was convinced that she wanted to marry *him*. Her husband was a three-martinis-at-lunch drunk who now could barely keep his eyes open in public. With Dan, Joyce was always going on about the men who were "after her," like the book salesman who, she said, had asked her to "run off" with him. Dan thought she was planting suggestions for the two of them. He doubted that any men wanted to "run off" with Joyce or would stay with her if they did. She was too homely, too hyper, too . . . odd. No wonder her husband drank all the time.

And now, here she is coming toward him across the dining room in the London Hilton, forty-seven years after those anguished and hateful notes, the threatened lawsuits over "death threats" from both sides, the early memoirs, the middle memoirs, the retaliatory fictionalized short stories (three by him, two hundred twelve by her). They have finally agreed to meet after all these years, Dan's partner of many years incapacitated and in a home, Joyce's two husbands dead and cremated and resting in separate urns on the mantel back at one of her homes in the States.

Joyce has aged surprising well. In fact at seventy-nine she looks better than she did at thirty-two. She's wearing her now-gray hair in a bun at the back. The skin of her small skull is tight, a few wrinkles at the edges of her eyes, which are huge and hungry, like those of pathetic, orphaned children in ads, only on Joyce the eyes look wild rather than frightened. She has become Jewish since he last saw her. While doing research for a novel, she discovered that her grandparents, from Hungary, had converted to Catholicism to escape the Holocaust. She has written extensively about it. She is tall and has excellent posture as she strides into the dining room, wearing an expensive-looking dark red coat, her large black leather purse slung across her shoulder. She spots him at the table, waiting.

I must look fat, Dan suddenly thinks. Certainly I'm no longer lean, still tall, only an inch shorter at seventy-nine, but in no way lean. He has filled in with the years, full of resentments and grudges and broken friendships and desserts. His pleasant face is still youthful, and he's had a facial just for this reunion with Joyce. He thinks it gives him a glow that he hasn't had for some time. His teeth are perfect and his mind still clever.

They greet each other by name. He stands, but they do not embrace. He lets her remove her coat herself, remembering how she flicked her finger dismissively at his hand when he tried to help her with another coat, the day, years before, when he had told her with trepidation, over lunch, that he was gay. He wonders if she remembers that.

"I'm so glad you agreed to come today," Dan says.

"It's such a lovely view," Joyce says, looking out the window at Park Lane.

"I was sorry to hear about your second husband's passing," Dan says as he sits.

"Oh, did you ever meet him?" she says, abruptly shutting off her cell phone after one ring and pushing it next to the centerpiece of poinsettias and miniature chandeliers. The white tablecloth is immaculate.

"No, I'm sorry I never did," Dan says.

"I don't think you two would have gotten along," Joyce replies.

The waiter, in tails, is waiting by a nearby archway to see if they look ready to order. But they aren't. A bus person, from India perhaps, pours water for them both into their large crystal glasses.

"We've come a long way," Dan says, gesturing at their elegant surroundings. He can feel the tailored suit with vest that he just had made encircling his body, keeping him warm. He has never quite fully adjusted to the British weather, even though he has now lived in England, mainly the Lake District, for many years.

"It's too bad we quarreled all those years ago," Joyce says. She touches the brooch on her lilac-colored blouse. "I suppose we lost a good friendship." She flicks her eyes across his.

"Maybe we would have tired of each other," Dan says. "Just like an old married couple."

"Do you think so?" She seems obsessed with her brooch, keeps fingering it. It is a cheetah or maybe a serval, some kind of large cat, made of black and gray agate, the eyes diamonds.

"I like your brooch," Dan says. He pronounces it *bruuch*, as a joke.

She laughs. "That's so you," she says.

"Don't want to forget my peasant roots," he says. He remembers half a century earlier when she corrected him at lunch when he said "I'm full." "Nice people say they are *finished*," she'd said. Her father had been a middle-class diemaker, Dan's a factory worker. The nervous bus person looks to re-fill their water glasses, but neither Dan nor Joyce has taken so much as a sip yet. The waiter, an elegant, thin, blond man from Eastern Europe, steps forward to take their order. "Are you ready?" he asks, in impeccable English. "Or not?" He wouldn't dream of rushing them.

"I'll just have the arugula salad," Joyce says. "And water."

"Oh, please order a full meal," Dan says. "I'm paying!" He remembers back when they were young instructors at a Catholic university in Detroit. She always liked him to leave the tips. "Men like to pay," she was fond of saying. I *hated* paying those tips, Dan thinks.

"I hear that another play of yours is a big hit in New York," Joyce says.

"Can't complain," he says. "But I will!" He laughs. "They just keep flowing out of my pen. It just took time for the world to catch up."

"I never much liked the theater," Joyce says.

"I remember," Dan says. "I'll have the filet mignon, well done," he says to the waiter.

"Anything else, sir?"

"No."

The waiter bows and goes off.

Joyce takes a long sip from her crystal water glass. "I've always regretted your asking for that favor all those years ago," she says, still holding the glass. Her fingers are old, claw-like, he notices, older than her face.

"Me too," he answers. "Considering that it 'destroyed our friendship.'"

Joyce's eyes grow wide. "I felt betrayed. I had won the National Book Award and everybody under the sun was after me, wanting things from me."

"Must have been horrible," Dan says, just barely hiding his sarcasm.

"I couldn't trust anybody. I thought I could trust you. You liked me before I became famous. And then came your note, begging for . . . What was it exactly you were begging for?"

"I asked you to see if your contacts at *The New York Times Book Review* might arrange a review of my novel, that angry gay protest novel."

"But you must have known that I couldn't review it. That's not how the *Times* works. They try very hard to prevent friends from reviewing books."

"I did not expect *you* to review it. I was asking if your contacts could at least get it into a reviewer's hands."

"Hadn't I already given a blurb? 'Engrossing, powerful, and disturbing.' Wasn't that it? Yes, I remember writing it, at the prompting of Blanche."

Blanche had been their literary agent at the time.

"I found out later that back then any review of anything gay, if it appeared at all, was required by the paper's publisher to be negative. So maybe it was a good thing no review ever appeared."

"Negative? I doubt that."

"The publisher's admitted it years later, in his memoirs." Dan sips his water.

"Did he?"

"I suppose I shouldn't have put all my eggs in one basket."

"I never did. Believe me, as a woman writer, I never let myself be that vulnerable. Hence my so-called 'excessive violence.'" Dan forces a smile. Joyce had never, he felt, had a day when she wasn't sought out, lionized, repeatedly published, interviewed, marveled over, and had smoke blown up her ass BECAUSE she was a "woman writer."

"Shall we say the gay movement was not quite as welcomed as the women's movement was?"

"But gay is everywhere now." She toasts him with her water glass.

"It wasn't then," he says flatly. "Somehow we had to get from there to here." He toasts her back.

"Yet you chose to write about that!" Joyce's small face looks annoyed as she tilts her head to one side.

"I chose to write about it because you weren't allowed to write about it." He keeps his voice very low and steady. His new suit itches.

"Well, we write about what we must, I suppose." Again she looks out at Park Lane.

"You never were quite on board with my subject matter, were you?" Dan is trying his best to seem lighthearted about it, but he is failing.

"I didn't? Well, I got your dirty novel published, didn't I?"

He gulps. "*I* got my novel published!"

"Well, you used my agent."

"You weren't Blanche's only client. I was just another one of her clients."

"She became your agent because you were a friend of mine."

"I thought she liked my book. She said she did."

"She asked me about your angry novel – what I thought. She wasn't even sure that she should represent it."

"This is the first I've heard of this." He wants a drink of water but is afraid he might spill some on the perfect tablecloth.

"She felt it was too graphic in some of the sex scenes."

"It was tame. I'm sure any gay sex seemed 'too graphic' at the time."

"I told her you would be heartbroken if she turned it down."

"You told Blanche Gregory to take on my novel?"

"And she did, and she sold it to G.P. Putnam on the fourth try. Right?"

"I thought she took it on because she thought it said something that needed to be said about oppression."

She gives a little laugh. "Oh, Dan, you're so naive. You were naive then, and you still are."

"Why didn't you tell me this before?"

"Because I thought your feelings would be hurt."

"No, they wouldn't have been." He knows that they would have been, crushed in fact. "Maybe I wouldn't have asked you to help with a review if I had known all this."

"Oh, I doubt that you would have been satisfied. You saw me as a meal ticket or some such. You expected me to . . ." She literally throws up her hands.

"I was bringing out a subject that had been in the dark for ages! I was helping to change the world!" He knows he sounds pretentious.

"Oh, who reads gay novels?!" she snaps. "Are you kidding? I was just not interested in the subject."

"You made me have to hide some of the most important aspects of myself. Not that you were the only one."

"You kept wanting to thrust it in my face. I don't how many times I had to steer the conversation away from that topic. I could tell you were itching to 'spill the beans,' and all over my lunch. I thought you were extremely insensitive in trying to force your lifestyle on me when I did not want to indulge in it."

"But I was bursting, dying to share myself with you, with anybody!"

"Oh, for God's sake, Dan, do you think I didn't know you were gay?"

"You knew I was gay?!"

"Not at first. But very soon. Do you think my husband would've let me go out with you so much if you were straight?"

"But you said that Ray was going to shoot me one day because he feared I'd take his wife away from him."

"Oh, that was merely a joke. The first time he met you, afterwards he said, "I think your friend Dan is a 'friend of Dorothy.'"

"He did not! There was nothing gay about me in the least!"

"Old movies, secretiveness, always looking at men, always wanting to 'share' some horrible secret that I didn't want to share, opera!"

"I've never liked opera and you know it. And as for my 'horrible secrets,' you could write about your own 'secrets,' your adulterous escapades, your rape fantasy crap, every disgusting thing you could dredge out of that swamp you call your brain. But not me! Not me!"

"I guess more readers like my 'swamp' than like yours." She seems very confident, not the least bit afraid.

"Do you still carry a pistol?" he asks her.

"I'll let you guess."

His eyes go to her purse hanging from the back of her chair.

"Have you come here to shoot me?" He smiles.

"So melodramatic, Dan." She smiles as well.

"I thought that you had agreed to meet with me today because you had remorse about the way you treated me, the way you chose to dismiss my desperation all those years ago."

"I thought you had agreed to meet to apologize to me for betraying our friendship." She looks off to the side.

"I was actually hungry when I reached out to you with that note. Literally."

"You shouldn't have linked it to *The New York Times,* asking me to risk my relationship there. Perhaps if I had known you were hungry, I could have scraped up a check."

"You were already a millionaire by then. But no check necessary. You could have gone out to lunch with me for that year and paid the tips. At least your *own!*"

"Is it always money with you, Dan?" She looks like she might be going to have one of her panic attacks.

"If it was only money, I wouldn't have written on the topics I did."

She hesitates. "You were never that good a novelist, you know that now, don't you?"

"How am I supposed to answer that?"

"I'm not trying to be mean. Maybe you're better now. I haven't seen your plays."

"You're too kind."

"That book was bad! You don't know that?! So preachy! It would never have been published if it weren't about homosexuals."

"And don't you imagine that your novels are published because they are about heterosexuals? And when you write about homosexuality you always link it with torture and rape!" He throws his napkin on the table. "You don't know the first thing about the subject except your own ridiculous fantasies!"

"You mustn't be jealous of me, Dan. It is beneath you."

He looks at her purse hanging from the back of her chair. What if he grabbed it, got Joyce's pistol, and shot her? And then himself? He has been having such impulsive thoughts of late, probably losing control of part of his brain.

"We'll see who time is good to, as writers," he says. "Whose books are read in the future." He smiles wickedly. "You may just be a footnote in my biography, an irritant who made me strong."

Joyce looks out at Park Lane again through the window. "Oh, you mean in the future, when nobody reads books at all?"

They finish the lunch, pay separately, and never speak again. Joyce Carol Oates goes on to be short-listed many times for the Nobel Prize in Literature but never wins it. Daniel Curzon never wins, it either.

Neither one kills the other, and that is the happy ending of this story.

FIRE BAD?

THEY HAD AGREED years before not to smoke in their apartment. Yin, eighty, was allowed to smoke in the bathroom if he opened the window, or on the fire escape. He was the only smoker of the two. Yin was skinny with a wrinkled butt and bad posture. He loved to be depressed. He had smoked forever, even in the womb. He liked to push everything to the edge, to see what he could get away with.

Yang, ninety, was corpulent and self-absorbed, a maker of chessboards by hand. His vice was caffeine. He did not like most people, but he also hated to be alone.

One dark, cold night Yang got up to see if the toilet was still clogged. It was. He tried a few thrusts with the plunger, to no avail. His arms hurt. He poured some more Drano into the toilet bowl. As he left the bathroom, he thought he smelled smoke. He walked down the hall, dressed in just half his pajamas (the bottom half) and looked at Yin's bed (the couch in the living room) and could not see him. They had not slept in the same bed for years.

Out of the corner of his eye in the darkness, Yang could see a lighted cigarette. "Yin?" he asked.

There was no reply.

"Are you smoking?"

"Yes," said Yin.

"You know this is a no-smoking apartment!"

"Fuck you," said Yin.

"Fuck you!" Yang countered.

"It's too cold in the bathroom with the window open."

"You are going to burn us both to death." Yang gestured at the silhouettes of all the piles of "my stuff" that Yin had "stored" everywhere in the living and dining rooms.

Yin's answer was a puff on his glowing cigarette.

"If there is a fire at night, you won't be able to find your way out, you know that, don't you?"

"Fuck you."

"The toilet is still clogged. Can you try the plunger?"

"Fuck you." The light of the cigarette was defiant.

Yang went back to bed and pulled the comforter over his head.

During the night, a fire from Yin's second cigarette set some old magazines on fire. He sat on his couch nodding from his various medications, both legal and illegal, and he did not wake up until he felt his crotch burning. By then it was too late. He went into shock, inhaled smoke, and burned to death where he sat.

Yang, a heavy sleeper, heard nothing. When he awoke in the morning, he was sorry to see his life-long partner burnt to death. But now at last he could get rid of all the trash in the living and dining rooms. And the Drano had done wonders on the toilet clog.

HAVING IT ALL

HYPA HAD BEEN born black. She did not want to be black, but there was nothing she could do about it. Hypa was a cat.

She felt that the other cats looked down on her because of the color of her fur. They all had light fur or spotted fur or anything but black fur. There were even rumors of Satanists kidnapping and mistreating black cats in rituals on Halloween. Hypa became very defensive and even developed an Attitude. She hissed and showed her sharp claws to one and all. She strutted around the 'hood where she lived, her triangular nose in the air, her yellow eyes flashing. Some of the other residents felt sorry for her, but most did not like her one bit. She had been seen on more than one occasion tormenting mice in a dumpster. It wasn't just the usual killing of mice that was considered normal and healthy by the residents but some downright cruel stuff. Best not to spell it out. Most wrote her off as "feral."

Hypa spent her days not looking for a job. "They wouldn't hire me anyway," she reasoned. "Besides, they're hiring all those fucking Siamese!" The Siamese were thought to be smarter and more hard-working than the other types of cat. So Hypa kept body and soul together by selling illegal drugs to white suburban cats, who sneaked into Hypa's 'hood – catnip mostly. She was also known to be good for some heroin bubbles that you could buy in a bottle with a blower, but you had to order two weeks in advance. Hypa got pregnant three times by the time she was two, but she went to some sleazy back-alley place and had the pregnancies "taken care of." One of her babies somehow escaped the "doctor" in the back alley and found his way home and came to live with his mother. He was black, white, and autistic.

He didn't fit in with the other kittens in the 'hood, and Hypa worried about him. Every once in a while, she'd give him a lick across the top of his head. But she had to leave him by himself much of the time. You see, she had to go out to catch lunch and dinner every single day. She tried to get her baby (Latavius) to go hunting with her, but he didn't want to. Hypa was growing afraid that her child was not only autistic but gay and vegetarian. "If you are a vegetarian," she warned him, "I'll never speak to you again. You hear me?"

He heard her, but Latavius pretended he didn't. Instead, he played with a wadded-up piece of paper in the garage where they lived. Best not to know what was inside that wadded-up paper. Sometimes Hypa and Latavius watched birds from the one window inside the garage. Their mouths would chatter simultaneously as the sparrows and robins flitted about on the tree outside. At those times Hypa thought maybe her son would turn out all right after all. She had great hopes for her child even though those for herself were growing dim by age three. "You can be anything you put your mind to," she told him often. "Even President of the United States."

"I don't think I want to be President," Latavius said.

"Then you can be Vice President," she encouraged.

"Are you President of the United States?" he asked her.

"No. Play with that wadded-up piece of paper I gave you."

Their lives went on, day by day, except for that one day when Hypa did not come home from hunting. Her son became distraught and meowed pitifully. One of the neighbors reported the noise, and Animal Control came out in a great big, threatening SUV and looked around. Luckily, Latavius hid behind some old tires in the garage and the Animal Control people didn't find him.

He knew he had to find his mother or he would starve, so Latavius set off the next morning to look for her. His belly was hurting and he was also worried about her. He had many, many adventures (elaborated upon in the memoir he later wrote but not relevant here). Eventually, he found his mother, and it was just as he had feared. Hypa was dead now and barely recognizable. Yet underneath the slushy snow he knew it was his late mommy. He attempted to lift her off the side of the road where she was splayed out, but he couldn't budge her. She looked awful, her yellow eyes open but terribly dimmed, her tongue lolling out of her mouth. He hoped that she had not suffered. "Did you suffer, Mommy?" he asked.

Hypa did not answer.

After an hour, he left her where she lay. He prayed that the City would give her a decent burial. He crawled back to the garage they had shared and somehow found the strength and the wits to start fending for himself. He stayed out of the drug world, thank God, and discovered soy mice at a health food store that threw out a lot of its expired stock in the back. Latavius grew up on his own, strong, together, optimistic, and American.

Latavius did not become President of the United States, but he was appointed to a Cabinet-level position under the first Green Party President – as Director of the Office of Management and Budget. You see, in America you can be ANYTHING you can dream of being, even if you're a feral cat with autism.

TRASH TALK

TITUS ("BONECRUSHER") Jones was about to go into the octagon against Fedor ("Repulsive") Goolagolov, two light heavyweights. But first they had to have a weigh-in the day before. Jones stood on the scale at 6'4", 205 pounds, well muscled and belligerent. He had to remove his trunks to make weight. His huge man-member swung free just out of the TV camera's range. Goolagolov stood 5'9", 204 pounds, skin-headed and sneering, a long scar near his lower lip. His ordinary-sized man-member could not be seen inside his trunks. Next, they stood face to face with their fists held up to intimidate each other. It was a pose.

"I'm going to ground and pound you until you squeal," threatened Jones. "First round and you're gone."

"No, I supmit you with kimura," snarled Goolagolov. With his heavy Russian accent, it was sometimes hard to understand him. For those who do not understand MMA lingo, a kimura is a behind-the-back arm twist on an opponent. The opponent could wind up with a broken arm if he doesn't tap or get free. It is named after the great Japanese jiu-jitsu fighter, Masahiko Kimura.

The press wanted to know what Goolagolov thought of Jones's MMA abilities.

"Him big pussy!" the Russian champion said. "I fuck him, then keel him!"

"And what do you think of 'Repulsive?' the press pressed.

"I'm gonna make him eat out my ass," replied Jones, dancing around the stage.

"What he say?" Goolagolov asked a reporter.

"He says he's going to make you eat out his ass" came the explanation.

"He will suck my dick, big time!" Goolagolov patted the front of his trunks.

The promoter, who stood between them looking red-faced, overweight, and pleased, said, "That's enough trash talk, you two."

But Jones was not about to quit. "Then I'm going to squirm on top of his cock until it turns purple."

"Vhat is *burple*?" Goolagolov wanted to know.

"I'm going to take my time and make it really hurt," Jones answered.

"I get arm bar and make him buck up and down like heifer while I laugh like spotted hyena." The Russian ha-haed.

"Let's see him escape my rear naked choke!" Jones gloated, demonstrating the choke. His muscled arms rippled and his man-member swayed.

"I twist his tits!" Goolagolov exulted.

"That's not allowed," somebody in the press corps said.

"I not care! I twist! He bawl like baby!"

"If he does, then I'm gonna squeeze his nut sack," Jones countered.

"That's not permitted, except in Russia," somebody clarified.

"I cannot crush his nut sack in this country?!" Goolagolov exclaimed, very disappointed.

"I will inflict a triple Salchow on him!" Jones said.

"That's figure skating," somebody explained.

"It is?" Jones said, surprised. "I never watch figure skating! It's too gay!"

The Salchow is named after the great Swedish skater Ulrich Salchow, who may or may not have been gay.

"You guys!" said the promoter, eating a snack: three burritos, a chalupa, and fries. Three bosomy, pretty young women walked by, holding up signs. "How about those ladies?!" he cheer-led. "The lovely Tiffany, Johanna, and Audriana!" The ladies stuck out their bosoms, smiled seductively, and scampered back to their chairs on the side.

"See, no gays here!" the promoter said, pumping one fist into the air.

"Next I fist him, big time!" Goolagolov was saying. He placed his fist gently against Jones's cheek – a face cheek, that is. "Vhat you do then, huh?" he challenged Jones.

On and on they went, saying what they would do to each other. That is why Mixed Martial Arts is so popular with straight men. It's *so* NOT GAY.

LOOK ON MY WORKS, YE MIGHTY, AND DESPAIR

JEROME COMES from money. (I tell you this so that you probably won't like him. I am a little pissed with Jerome at the moment.) Jerome's father and mother are both rich through inheritance, his sister through marriage, but Jerome himself has very little money since his relatives keep theirs to themselves. (I tell you this so you may better understand Jerome.) Oh, they give him cash for a new food processor or cutlery set every now and again, hardly enough to notice. But of course Jerome does notice and is very resentful. He has always been a dutiful son and brother, but when it comes to money he is always low on their list of recipients. They think of him as a cook. He fumes silently, and sometimes not silently.

Jerome is a short man with a short fuse. He has thickened around his middle over the years and grown a white beard, but that is where the comparisons to Kris Kringle end. He is not jolly and he does not bring presents. Instead, he writes a snarky blog three days a week in which he comments on various aspects of life. He fancies himself something of a food expert and gets the occasional free meal from restaurants in return for coverage on his blog. He does not know the exact number of readers his blog has, but he is pretty certain it is over twenty. He has a tattoo of Oscar Wilde's face on the tip of his left index finger, the finger with which he says he types his "witty blog." He insists that Oscar was left-handed.

Here is an example of Jerome's French blog, from last week: "The Salade Niçoise at Joseph's is quite tasty, especially since Joseph's is a Palestinian restaurant and not a French. However, on its website, there is a terrible misuse of 'in regards to' for the correct 'in regard to' that can only distress the judicious diner."

And his latest just appeared: "The whipped potatoes at Legumes To Die For are an interesting side dish, but overall the food there is overpriced and AWFUL and should be left on the side."

Another friend of mine runs Legumes To Die For and must be devastated to read the entry.

"Somebody had to tell them," Jerome tells me. "At least *I* do it with wit." He wags his Oscar Wilde finger at me.

I haven't even been to that restaurant, so I merely nod vaguely.

I notice that Jerome has grown even thicker since I last dined out with him. He is also sporting a lavender bow tie and suspenders now. He orders his usual from the server: "Chilled cranberry juice dripped – not spilled – over crushed ice with a sprig of mint – on the bottom, not the side or the top of the glass. Do you understand?"

"I do, sir," the server replies, over-smiling.

Jerome tends to be curt with "help"of any sort, odd for one so Liberal.

"They so rarely get it right the first time," Jerome complains to me.

"You must have such sensitive taste buds," I say. (I don't believe Jerome catches my sarcasm.)

I'm no saint myself. I have no interest in food, the arts, movies, travel, news, or sports, not now that I am ninety-six. To tell the truth, I have never had much interest. But I am always nice to "help."

The server brings Jerome's drink to the table, and of course it is wrong. The sprig of mint lies on the side of the crushed ice, NOT on the bottom. "I can bring you another, sir," the server says.

"Do!"

"Does it really make that much difference?" I ask Jerome sincerely.

"There are some things in life one can, and must, control," he says brittely. "I also often get a second free drink this way. It is my form of art." He grins a Santa-like grin.

The next day Jerome emails me. "Did you see that terrible thing on Yelp?" he asks.

I never use the Internet if I can help it, so I haven't seen it. "What is it?" I ask.

Jerome sends this, copied from the business review website:

"Jerome of Jerome's Amusing Musings, a blog, is full of himself. That must be why he is so fat."

"Who wrote it?" I ask.

"Some blockhead!" Jerome says. "How dare they review me on Yelp! I am not a business!" You can taste the indignation in his voice.

"Will anybody notice?" I inquire.

"I may lose readers!" Jerome laments.

"Perhaps it will excite interest."

"If they think they can stop me from correcting their grammar, they are sadly mistaken!" Jerome says.

"I'm sure it will pass."

"No, once it's up on Yelp, it stays forever. It's the Internet!"

"Why don't you write to the operators of the website and request that the comment be removed?"

"I already have. Yelp refuses!"

"I can send in a favorable review of your blog," I offer.

"Would you? Oh, you're a godsend!"

I can see that it means a lot to Jerome, so I send in this: "Amusing Musings by Jerome is a fantastic website! But read it at your peril."

Immediately, Jerome emails me: "Why did you mention 'peril' in your comment?"

"Because I thought it would provoke interest."

"Well, there's no need to appeal to the lowest common denominator," he replies. "And my blog is called Jerome's Amusing Musings, not Amusing Musings by Jerome."

"I'm sorry. Do you want me to take it down?"

"Let's leave it up for a few days to see what happens."

I go back to my reading. I do a lot of reading these days (mostly histories of ancient fallen civilizations), even though my eyes are not good and whatever I read will die with my brain in the grave.

Jerome sends me his latest blog two days later, which includes this item: "Mercutio's features a Capulet and Montague soup made of tomato bisque on one side of the bowl and clam chowder on the other. A charming idea, but two drops of the Capulet were already spilled over into the Montague in my bowl and thus I was robbed of the delight of mixing the two soups myself."

I do not quite know how to respond. But I know Jerome is waiting for a response.

Before I can get back to him, he is on the phone. "Did you see Yelp?!" He sounds outraged.

"I'm afraid I haven't." I don't want to hear it.

"Here, let me read it to you." I wait while he finds it. "'Jerome may think his musings are amusing, but I find him to be a pretentious motherfucker!'"

"Does it really say that?"

"Well, it says 'MFer,' but we all know what that means." He sounds livid.

"Maybe the website will take it down because of the obscenity."

"I already emailed them. The answer is no. They are committed to free expression, they say."

"Well, fuck them," I nod sagaciously.

"Maybe you could reply yourself. Is there a place for that?"

"I wouldn't stoop to their level!"

"I could send in another nice review of your blog."

"Thanks, but I doubt that will help much. And your writing is sort of . . . "

I don't answer. Jerome does not seem to notice.

"I'd like to catch those bastards who are sending in those nasty comments about me!" Jerome seethes. "I'll eviscerate them with my pen."

"What will it matter in a thousand years?" I say.

"I care about now! *Now!* I get free theater tickets and restaurant meals because of my blog! Don't you understand that?! I could never afford these with my current income! If only my relatives weren't so stingy!"

"I understand," I sympathize.

"And I got another nasty comment today! It won't stop! It says this: 'Jerome of Jerome's Amusing Amusings is neither amusing nor museful.'"

"Oh, that's terrible," I commiserate.

Jerome cries. Actually cries. "Oh, another review is coming in," he says.

"Oh, no!" I exclaim.

"Can you believe this?!"

"What?"

"It says: 'Jerome's Amusing Musings must be written while he's on the toilet. They have the feel of strained turds.'"

"That's dreadful and unkind," I say.

"Who could say such terrible things about me?" Jerome weeps. "Especially when I'm so witty?!"

"Yes, who?" I say to him.

Yes, *who*? I say to you.

[Is this a work of fiction or payback?]

[Is there a difference?]

A SEARING MEMORY

IN RECENT WEEKS memories from my past have been flooding into my mind. Maybe it's because I've reached a landmark year in life. I can feel it in my bones, see it on the backs of my hands as I type this. I am also starting to forget things. Is it *i* before *e* except after *c*? Is Pluto a planet or not? Should you brush your teeth up and down or in a circle? I rarely brush mine anymore. I am not close to anyone, never kiss. I had an infection in my upper tooth, but it seems to have passed. So let that go, bad breath, good breath.

There is one memory that keeps coming back, and I want to deal with it. I have settled scores with several old friends and colleagues, sending letters telling them how much I hate them. I put my notes in Christmas cards, thus surprising them and doubling the poison. I made a vow many, many years ago that I would not let people get the better of me, not once if I could prevent it, certainly never twice.

Most people need to be liked. I'd rather be victorious.

That one memory that keeps returning is of the time I was seventeen, bookish, virginal, a little pimply, lanky, thin, needy. I was known at my Catholic school as one of the "good boys." I'd even won a trophy from the nuns for it. But in senior year I started hanging out with some of the "bad boys" in my class, much to the dismay of Sister Marie Ann, who thought I was destined to be a saint. "Stay away from those boys!" she cautioned me. "They will drag you to Hell!" But I was lonely, and so I kept going back, after I had done my homework, to the Sweet Shop, where the "bad boys" hung out. Only one of them actually liked me, Mike, I could tell. Unlike the others, Mike was nice, even though he was missing his front teeth from some football accident. He was spindly but athletic, smart but far from studious. He would go on to flunk out of community college after one semester. He laughed at my jokes, and I loved him for it. He had sort of a "girlfriend" named Carla, who hung around the Sweet Shop too, mostly to be around Mike. I was pretty sure she thought I was in competition with her for Mike. Maybe I was. This was a long time ago, and boys certainly didn't say they "liked other boys that way" back then. Did you want to be killed?

But it isn't Mike or Carla that keeps coming back in memories. I suppose they're both dead now, buried in the wastelands of Detroit, which they never left. I got out through a B.A., an M.A., and even a Ph.D. – as far away as education could take me. Rather, the memory is of Teddy Mowidd, who was a friend of Mike's, squat, bowlegged, with an early-fuzz mustache, and hair that he never combed, and a snotty, superior air that enveloped him, God knows why.

It may have been because I blinked a lot when I was seventeen, or maybe because he thought I had a "secret crush" on Mike. I don't think Teddy had a secret crush on Mike or anybody else. He was just mean. One of the things you learn in this life is that some people are just mean. Teddy would come into the Sweet Shop maybe twice a week. The Sweet Shop was hardly sweet. It had ugly brown linoleum on the floor, chipped ice cream dishes, and stools at the counter that had sections ripped out of them. We lived in a neighborhood that was on the way down, although we didn't fully understand yet that history was stomping on our faces.

I barely ever spoke to Teddy, maybe a grunted hello here and there. There are some people you dislike immediately. Teddy was one of those, at least for me. The others, some six or seven, seemed to accept him well enough.

One night Teddy and I were there alone. I was having a hot fudge sundae, trying to gain weight, believe it or not. He was having a cherry phosphate. He seemed bored and slouched around on his stool, which was at the other end of the soda fountain. I tried not to make eye contact with him and was hoping Mike or some of the others would stop by.

Suddenly, Teddy gets up from his stool and saunters toward me. "How's it going, blinky boy?" he asks me.

I probably mumbled "Not too bad" or something like that. I didn't have the guts to say anything to him. I did turn away, I remember that. I hurried through my hot fudge sundae and stood up to leave.

"Where you going?" Teddy wants to know.

"Home."

"Naw, sit back down. You want to see a trick?"

"Not particularly," I say.

"Oh, blinky boy here says 'not particularly' – like a good nun!" He laughs too loudly at his own joke and shoots a glance at Sam, the owner of the Sweet Shop. Sam was maybe forty-five then, but he seemed ancient to us kids. He had a limp and gave small scoops of ice cream and was letting the Sweet Shop go downhill. "Are you going to become a nun?" Teddy says, turning his wit on me again.

"I've got homework to do," I say. I had already done it, but I want to get away from Teddy.

"Naw, you gotta see this trick I know." He takes out a box of matches. "I bet you can't break a match with one finger," he says. Everybody smoked back then, even in Sweet Shops. The past is a foreign country, as somebody once said. I couldn't bring myself to leave. Protocol said that you had to stay and watch Teddy's trick and then tell him afterward how terrific it was.

"Here's how it goes," Teddy says. He grabs for my hand. I flinch.

"Hey, he flinched!" he says to Sam.

I let him continue.

"I'm not gonna hold your hand, blinky boy. Not to worry. I'm not Mike!" He thinks this is hilarious and almost bends in two from laughing so hard. "Give me your hand. I'm not gonna hurt you." I had taken my hand back. "I'm gonna arrange these two matches on the sides of the matchbox and then I'm gonna place another match across the top, like it's a bridge. And I bet you can't break that top match with just one finger. You right-handed or left?"

"Right."

He starts arranging the index finger and thumb of my left hand around the matchbox.

I think: I'll break the goddamned match and show him!

Teddy's fingers are unsteady, but finally he manages to put the third match across the two that are sticking up. "There!" he says. "Now let's see you break it. But just *one* finger, okay? Bet you can't do it!"

How weak does he think I am?! I curse to myself.

I bring the index finger of my right hand down hard onto the top match of the bridge that Teddy has built. It doesn't break, but the force of the blow does drag the matches down the two sides of the matchbox, far enough for them to catch fire. My thumb and finger are burned. Because of the sweat and the pressure, the two lit matches stick to my skin and burn me even longer. Teddy laughs and twirls around on his stool. Sam laughs a little bit too.

"Boy, are you dumb, blinky boy!" Teddy says, clapping me on the back.

I sit there stunned. I cannot believe that he has actually made me burn my own fingers.

Believe me, I tried to find Teddy Mowidd for years after I got out of high school, but he had disappeared. I was going to throw gasoline on him. And light it.

Then, after college, I learned that Teddy was in federal prison. He had scammed retirees out of their pensions. Something like that. I thought about visiting him in prison and spitting in his face in the Visitation Room. Maybe if I could shake hands somehow, I could set his fingers on fire?

I thought of writing a story about him and making him read it, if he could read, and seeing him groveling in remorse.

I found out that Teddy Mowidd died last week, the same age as me.

I thought about going to his grave and setting it on fire.

But I didn't. I realized that you can only change the past by forgiving it. So when I found out that he had a child, a boy with a major learning disability, now an old man, living in a mental hospital in northern California, I brought Teddy's grown child a yummy, pretty, frosted cupcake. Fuck.

THE EMPEROR'S SKIN

THERE ONCE LIVED a powerful Emperor who had very thin skin. I did not know this Emperor personally, as he lived many hundreds of years ago, and I am but a poor mortal man living now.

Yet his story has come down to us as a warning, which I pass on to you.

It was said that this Emperor was as tall as an oak tree, with flowing blond locks, and arms mighty with muscles. He had won the Emperorship by arm-wrestling many brave opponents to the death. His verbal skills were likewise immense, if ungrammatical, and he trumpeted his conquests without modesty of any kind, often standing on the corpses of the defeated and shaking his fists at all would-be opposition. He therefore struck fear into the hearts of all the People in his land, even though he had lost a lot of muscle tone of late and gone to lard in his chest and love-handles.

The Emperor had a beautiful wife from a foreign land with long, long hair, of a raven's color. Her name was Raven. She and the Emperor had sixteen children, as negotiated in their marriage deal, plus sixteen more from various earlier wives and concubines. The Emperor had set up his dynasty by naming his numerous children as his successors, in order of their birth. There were to be no more struggles for the throne because arm-wrestling for public office was now banned. The idea of an election by secret ballot was bruited about in the land for a while, but the People could not be bothered to participate in elections, and so the idea withered away. They much preferred the arm-wrestling, but now that was gone, too. The People grumbled, but they wouldn't vote, just grumble. Meanwhile, the Emperor, whose name was The Emperor, luxuriated in his high status and doled out plums to his many children every other day of the week, and twice on Sunday. "See how beautiful my children are!" proclaimed the Emperor. "They deserve these plums." They were indeed fine plums, greengages, mirabelles, and damsons. The Emperor's sons and daughters cross-bred some of their plums and made other deals in their vast dealings with other royalty from around the globe. They thought nepotism was a disease of the upper bowel.

The Emperor did not like to pay attention to the details of ruling his land and often slept through briefings from his counselors. He could barely read the large print, never mind the small, and preferred instead to issue proclamations on the spur of the moment. Various heralds, who were required to proclaim the proclamations, began to hate their jobs because they had to blare out "information" that was poorly researched and stunningly uninformed. They made the proclamations from Henry the Yeti, an earlier Emperor, seem like pearls from Aristotle. (They weren't. One of his was: "Me fuck bride before husband!") The People grumbled about the Emperor's favoritism toward his offspring, but all they did was grumble.

Although the Emperor loved to issue proclamations, even contradictory ones, he despised being contradicted. Now, nobody likes being contradicted, it must be said, but The Emperor, as I said earlier, had very thin skin. By that, I mean that, if so much as a syllable of contradiction of what he had said was vented anywhere by anyone, the Emperor would have his coterie of supporters seek out that person, have him or her deemed a Traitorous Felon, and then make him or her "disappear."

An example: One time a herald trumpeted the statistics on the popularity of everyone in the land. The herald, in the main town's main square, hear-ye'd that The Emperor was *second* in popularity. His lovely wife, Raven, who spoke only her native tongue, had come in first. The Emperor immediately had the herald flogged to death and then the lovely Raven was found strangled under a staircase. There were rumors that perhaps The Emperor had had something to do with his wife's untimely strangulation. But soon the Emperor married a new wife, a lovely ladies' maid from one of The Emperor's castles. Her name was Lovely. The People soon forgot the nasty rumors about the first wife's strangulation, so happy were they to celebrate a big wedding with free cake.

As he grew older, The Emperor seemed to grow stouter and more and more lardy. He had to have a whole new wardrobe made for him in XXXL size. Word soon reached The Emperor that the People were snickering at him behind his back. He was furious. "I'm as svelte and handsome as I was at twenty!" he shouted to one and all, at banquets, feasts, receptions, tea times, and brunches. "Hey, there goes Lard Ass!" someone in a crowd called out one day as The Emperor rode by on his steed, Magnificent. The Emperor immediately had the man arrested, tried, and executed that very day. "Call me Lard Ass, will you!" was his last word on the subject. The People grumbled against The Emperor and his imperious ways, but they said "We need a strong leader to lead us and to give us solutions for complicated socio-political issues beyond our ken."

The Emperor did not like to hear that the People were grumbling, even when it was pointed out to him that they in general approved of his reign. They liked the fact that he had built a Great Wall to keep out the invading Chinese and their shoddy, lead-filled goods. They liked the fact that he had driven vicious drug cartels back to Outer Los Angeles. They especially liked the registry of Jehovah's Witnesses. They hated the Jehovah's Witnesses.

The Emperor rose each morning wondering who had grumbled against him during the night. He had three of his bodyguards waterboarded and scalped because he thought they had smirked at his shrunken pee pee as he sat on his potty. He could barely have sex with his new wife without thinking, "Her grunts of satisfaction are not what they once were. They are her way of finding fault with my love-making." He had her tarred but not feathered, out of a last-minute surge of mercy. She was, however, banished.

"What makes our Emperor so thin-skinned?" was heard throughout the land.

"I think he was deeply sunburned as an infant," someone offered.

"I heard that he was dipped in the baptismal font at his christening and called 'this child of God,' and that made him afraid of any criticism ever since," said another.

"We're running out of compliments!" lamented many more.

Then one day, as The Emperor was scalding a latrine servant who had dared to say the Emperor's shit stank, the Emperor slipped and fell into the latrine itself. It was full, shall we say, for The Emperor sat there many times a day, excreting as he thought up his many proclamations. The Emperor clutched at the edge of the latrine, but he could not get a proper hold in order to lift himself out. His hands became slippery with his own offal, and the ooze in the latrine clung to the thin skin all over his fat body and burned through in a trice. Even though the scalded latrine servant tried to help The Emperor out of his unfortunate "bath," he lost his grip and thus was unable to, and The Emperor died screaming in agony as he sank from sight.

One of the Emperor's children took over the throne and threw a big coronation/wedding party, and the People were thrilled and danced and danced for days. Oh, and eventually they voted, around thirty-six percent overall.

[Criticizing the People is not about to get you many fans.]

[I can't help myself, said the old writer.]

SCROOGE REVISITED

NOT THAT LONG AGO, there was a man named Adolph Scrooge, a ruthless financial titan connected with the Nazis. He was a stooped, surly, little old man who overworked his employees and wouldn't give them any days off, even Christmas. He had no friends, except the Nazis, no social life, no sex, even with call girls, and kept his forty-seven-room mansion both shabby and drafty. He ran several sweat shops. The market for sweat for customers who couldn't make their own was big back then.

One night in his solitary, canopied, four-poster bed, the old gentleman was visited by three Spirits. For those who don't believe in Spirits, the visions may just have been inspired by the indigestion brought on by the gruel he'd had at his late, solitary dinner in his cold, drafty mansion.

The first Spirit, who was some kind of angel with its head on fire, kept pointing to people in Adolph's past: his sister, an old girlfriend, a younger, cuter version of himself, a former boss, etc.

"Why are you showing me these people?" Adolph asked. "I couldn't care less!"

The second Spirit was large and plump and decorated in all sorts of green velvet, with wreaths in its hair, even two in its beard. It showed Scrooge current holiday celebrations: one with his employee Bog Snatchitt and Bog's family, at which there was quite a bit of arguing over the small portions of goose the over-populating Snatchitt family were about to devour. An older sibling pushed the youngest away from the plate of goose and whacked him hard with a goose leg across the mouth and sent the boy, Big Timmy, who was overweight and developmentally disabled, crashing to the hard floor of the tiny Snatchitt hovel. The Spirit also showed Adolph his only living relative, his nephew, Freddy

Two Shoes, who set a place for his Uncle Adolph every Christmas even though he never showed up. The nephew was a moderate Whig and felt sorry for his rich but lonely uncle. No thought of being in his uncle's will ever crossed his mind.

The third Spirit, who arrived when Adolph's grandfather's clock struck three A.M., was skeletal and hooded with long, bony fingers and spoke not a word. By merely pointing, it revealed awful, possibly upcoming events in the rich man's life: his lonely death in his canopied bed, his bedclothes ripped off and stolen by Goodwill, and other horrors too horrible to recall. But one of them was a large crutch by a cold fireplace without the presence of the over-sized, developmentally disabled boy (Big Timmy) who had once owned it.

"Tell me, O Spirit, are these the Things to Come?" asked Scrooge.

"Yes, unless you change your selfish ways," replied the Third Spirit. "Mend your ways! Mend your ways, Adolph!" the Spirit called out as it flew away into the place where Spirits fly away to.

Adolph tossed and turned in his bed, unable to sleep, wracked with worry and concern, until, finally, he heard the sound of gentle snowflakes falling on the ground outside his mansion. (Adolph, be it noted, despite his age, had excellent hearing.) He got up to use the chamber pot next to the bed and through a window caught a glimpse of a lad he recognized from a nearby street. Adolph liked the look of the lad as he stood there with a morning woody – Adolph, not the lad. He rushed to the window and threw up the sash and called, "Hey, lad, I'll give you this big silver coin if you'll do me a favor!"

The lad was dubious and tugged at his scarf. "What do you want me to do?" he asked.

"Heads or tails. You choose!"

"Will it take very long?"

"It'll be over before you know it. By the way, how old are you, lad?"

"I'm fifteen."

"I think that's legal in Angola. We'll pretend we're in Angola. Come on up!"

Some say the lad went on up and some say he did not. It's up to you and how you like your Christmas stories. Okay, okay, the kid was twenty-one and Questioning!

ALTERNATE ENDING: Scrooge got up, trembling from the cold in his mansion, to brush his teeth with ashes from the fireplace and caught a glimpse of a lad he recognized from a nearby street. He liked the look of the lad and rushed to the window and threw up the sash and called, "Hey, boy, I'll give you this big silver coin if you do me a favor! I think I'm sick."

"What do you want me to do? Do you want that big turkey that's still hanging in the butcher shop window, to share with your only nephew and his family?"

"No, I'm a vegan. I want you to go to the Animal Rescue Place three streets over and get me a cat and bring it back."

"I don't think they're open on Christmas," said the lad.

"Ring the bell and tell them Adolph Scrooge will give them a large donation next Monday."

The lad scampered off with the big silver coin in his mittened hand and did not steal it and performed his errand. He rang the bell of the Animal Rescue Place, they answered, and he brought back a sweet little kitten with white spots on its front paws.

"You aren't going to eat this kitten for Christmas, are you?" the lad asked, his cheeks freezing.

Adolph Scrooge thanked the lad and then put the kitten in his bed, and its warmth plus his faint warmth in just ten minutes saved them both.

Oh, and though he didn't make up with his nephew, he did divest his portfolio of his Nazi holdings.

BONDED

THALIA AND DELIA were conjoined twins who were now five years old. They could have been separated at birth (in the conjoined sense), but the doctors were afraid one of them might die. They shared a liver and had but three legs. Thalia was the more dominant of the two because she faced forward while Delia faced Thalia's ear. So Delia couldn't actually control where they went, but she did have Thalia's ear.

They saw an ice skating program on TV and decided they wanted to learn to ice skate. This was complicated by the fact that they lived in Milpitas, California with its temperate climate, plus the twins being conjoined.

"Maybe you should wait until you two are separated," their (single) mother suggested.

"When will that be?" Thalia and Delia said as one.

"I want to do a quad," Thalia said.

"I want to do a back flip," said Delia.

For those who don't know, a "quad" is four twirls in the air, difficult for anyone to do, even if not conjoined. A back flip you probably know.

How the other children at the Special Needs Nursery laughed at Delia and Thalia. "You can't even walk!" said Lucius, who had learned to sign his name with his left foot. He had no right foot.

Lucius was perky and had appeared in several ads for St. Jude's Hospital and the Shriners.

"We can too!" said Delia and Thalia, about the ice skating.

Their single mother appeared on TV and cried because her little "angels" couldn't ice skate. Somebody set up a Go Fund Me account, and soon the twins had ninety-eight thousand sixty-six dollars for ice skates. However, when they bought the three ice skates they required, they discovered, at the ice rink they rented, that they fell down when they attempted the quad. They even fell down when they simply attempted to skate in the same direction. Their (single) mother encouraged them from the bench on the sidelines. They had come in an ambulance, which was still waiting for them when they wished to return home. "We're not leaving the ice rink until we've done a quad!" said the feisty twins, together.

How the other skaters in the rink laughed at them! And even called them names!

But they were plucky little things and came every day to practice. Their (single) mother always accompanied them and cheered them on. She did not have to work because of the Go Fund Me account. Sometimes she brought cocoa for the twins.

Within a year, the twins had learned to negotiate the ice and make it halfway around before they fell down. They got some bruises on their three legs.

The doctors concluded that, despite their hopes and some new technologies, they would not be able to separate the twins after all. They would have to live as they were and would probably live into their sixties. The twins were at first disappointed not to be separated, but then they realized that they would never be lonely, as so many are, and they would keep trying to learn to ice skate. They never conquered the quad or the back flip, but they did perfect a hop where the skater had to land on three legs, and it was given the official name of Thalia-Delia, which they alone could perform.

Then how the other skaters loved them!

THE TEN COMMANDMENTS ARE ONLY A ROUGH DRAFT

I. I AM THE LORD THY GOD. THOU SHALT NOT HAVE STRANGE GODS BEFORE ME

Helen Jarvis regularly watched the Public Broadcasting Service (PBS) news because it was widely considered the most factual, most reliable, and least partisan news broadcast around. As she was using her treadmill to keep her thirty-nine-year-old body in shape and stimulating the blood flow to her already red cheeks (from a touch of rosacea), she enjoyed the healthy sweat that infiltrated her sweat-suit and kept off the depression she always felt right behind her blue, bright eyes. She and her Irish Setter, the ironically named Redneck, also ran two miles a day in their suburban area and neither had, so far, been robbed or raped by some man jumping out of the bushes. Helen worked from her home, a lovely, very tidy, two-and-half bath, three-bedroom colonial. True, she was a bit lonely at times, but she worked so much she hardly noticed. She attended the services of the local Unitarian Universalist church.

One day, as she was Googling the meaning of "extrapolate," one of those words she kept forgetting the meaning of, Helen happened upon a link to a website that said: WHY TED BUNDY KILLED. She had never actually followed that particular serial killer's story (there being so many), but for some reason she clicked on the Ted Bundy story. Lots of ads popped up, all but overwhelming the computer screen. But Helen managed to get past the ads, even one that screamed that she had MALWARE on her computer. She had learned that those alerts about malware were usually malware themselves and best avoided. She read about all the women Ted Bundy had killed and went back to her own work (for Boeing, Accounts). She took an extra hour for lunch (Boeing wouldn't know) and found herself, in between bites of salami and Swiss cheese, Googling again. The Ted Bundy story had unnerved her somewhat and so she didn't enter any search words about him or serial murderers.

Instead, Helen clicked on a side link that said: PRISON ROMANCE. She had hesitated at first, thinking it might be some gay porn site, which was not her cup of tea. It turned out to be brief stories about young women of good breeding and upstanding character who encountered tall, difficult men with mysterious pasts who possessed large fortunes and turned out to be of royal blood. Sort of Jane Austen but for the busy modern woman.

Helen found herself spending more and more time on this website, even on ones that were merely linked to it, like EDWARDIAN LOVE TRIANGLES, FAIR LADIES OF THE BELLE EPOCH, and HE WOULDN'T KISS HER LADYSHIP. She began getting behind in her own accounting work and got several reprimands from Boeing. She now attended services at the Unitarian Universalist church only occasionally.

Alas, Helen couldn't stop going to these websites. They thrilled in her ways she didn't even know she could be thrilled. The hours flew by and she seemed to enjoy her Red Baron single-serve, fat-free pizzas even more as she watched. She had never been so happy in her life and the depression was all but gone.

Sad to say, Helen became ever and ever more dependent on these romance websites and couldn't stop herself. She stopped reading anything else and turned down two dates from two men she met at the required in-person days she had to spend at Boeing. They didn't look the least bit like they were of royal blood. Needless to say, she did no work for Boeing at all and was fired. She stopped attending services at the Unitarian Universalist church altogether.

When the authorities found Helen's body, she was draped over the keyboard of her computer, dead of a stroke, but her body very well toned – from the treadmill. Her dog, Redneck, had stood by her dead body for seven days. He was adopted by another employee at Boeing (in Sales).

Thus the Lord God was as right as He was righteous: Thou shalt not worship *false gods*!

***

Helen had a twin brother, fraternal, of course, but similar to his sister in appearance. At thirty-nine, Vernon had strong legs from running on the track at his gym, tight abs, slightly underweight (from watching those calories and avoiding sweets). He didn't look a day over thirty-eight.

He lamented the passing of his sister, Helen, although they hadn't been that close in recent years, what with his job in Sustainability (at AT&T) and her obsession with romance websites. He was *un*happily married with two brats that he had fathered. He often thought of running off to Azerbaijan or somewhere.

Then one day as he was looking up something online about "building trust in a shrinking world," Vernon saw a link to a news story: CROCODILES INVADE MIAMI SWIMMING POOLS. Vernon had never been to Miami and didn't know anybody there, but he was intrigued and clicked on the link.

It was a story about ten-foot-long crocs finding their way to unattended swimming and wading pools in Florida and snatching toddlers. There were even pictures of open croc mouths about to crunch down on unsuspecting children. There were some "Aftermath" pictures showing blood spots and bits of toddler clothes beside a wading pool. ARE YOU AND YOURS NEXT? the last line read. Oh, my God, Vernon thought, what if those crocs got my kids! He was a bit unsettled by the fact that the idea didn't upset him as much as he thought it should.

He clicked on another NEWS STORY.

This was about how badly certain movie stars of the past had aged. There was a slide show, amidst the multiple advertisements, of Brigitte Bardot, Dr. Ruth Jack Nicholson, and others, looking terrible right next to pictures of them in their youth. It's a warning to us all, Vernon thought. (What that warning was was a little vague in his mind: a warning not to get old?) Vernon found himself spending more and more time online, neglecting his wife and kids, doing shoddy work for AT&T on sustainability. (He was supposed to have finished a pamphlet on "Our Future Promise" months ago.)

But he had never felt so energetic and heady. He began each morning with such hope in his heart. He went to bed every night satiated and yet yearning for sunrise. He knew there were websites that made the world in all its magic available to Vernon's fingertips, keeping him alert, inspired, and knowledgeable:

PRESIDENT KEEPS DINOSAURS IN PRIVATE ZOO AMELIA EARHART FOUND ALIVE IN BRAZILIAN JUNGLE DEMOCRAT HOAX IN WIDESPREAD VOTER FRAUD UMPIRES CAUGHT IN SEX ORGIES BANKS BELLY UP IN CAIMAN ISLANDS JUNGLE FUNGUS KILLS BRAIN CELLS MIRACLE FUNGUS CURES CANCER LOSE FIFTY POUNDS VOTING REPUBLICAN.

Vernon suspected that perhaps some of these websites were suspect. Yet he didn't care. He felt so alive, he could even put up with his mean kids and boring job. He could have gone to Snopes, Fact Check, and Politifact to verify what was true, but he found them dull. He'd rather worship at other (strange and even fake) altars, like his sister.

II. THOU SHALT NOT MAKE ANY GRAVEN IMAGE NOR BOW DOWN AND WORSHIP IT

SERITA AND DIRK were lawfully wedded Millenials who wanted to have a family. They were trying very hard to make it happen: sex three times a day, four times one Sunday. They had no luck.

Serita thought it might be because she was very sensitive to light and loud noises. She was easy to cry and hated to be alone. She also was used by people, who often asked if they could stay for months in her house, and she always said yes. Dirk thought it might be because his wife had been married before to an illegal immigrant from El Salvador and hadn't used "protection." "It'll screw up your hormones," he said to everybody, except his wife.

Both were putting on some pounds and so they got checked out by their doctor, who said they were healthy but "should walk more." They did walk more, at least once, but they also drove their two cars a lot. They loved the waffle house downtown in their small city. They didn't drink alcohol, both being teetotalers and Christian, but they sure loved them waffles.

They hated their jobs, but they never came late. Serita kept medical records for several doctors, but only ones who wouldn't perform abortions. Dirk operated a package-delivery drone for Amazon.com, but it still had some kinks to be worked out. Mostly he worked on the drone itself. He was good with his hands.

They tried to get pregnant with fertility drugs but stopped before any of them were successful.

"They are forbidden by our religion," Dirk said. He was not sure that was true. He was really afraid that they might have a baby with three heads. He liked Freak Shows but not in his own family.

They had a period there where they thought they might be pregnant. Serita had missed her period. But it turned out to be some cream she used on her sensitive nipples. It had some side effects, like missed periods. She stopped using the cream.

Dirk bought a device online that promised to make his sperm "like Superman's," but it just turned his sperm blue, and that didn't seem so good.

They got to their mid-thirties with no children. They were both bummed out about it. Each got a raise and Serita's mom died and left them a nice house in Knoxville, Tennessee. They sold the house and added an extra room onto theirs. "It's for the babies," Serita said to the people who were staying with her and Dirk. That was her way of saying that when she got pregnant, they would have to leave.

However, she didn't get pregnant. Nor did Dirk. He did put on fifty pounds.

One day Serita came home a little late from work. Dirk was making a pot roast. She had gotten her first tattoo. "See what I got!" she laughed. "I hope you like it." She twirled around and showed him the small rose on the back of her wrist.

"Is it temporary?" Dirk wanted to know.

"Not really."

"Oh," he said flatly. He didn't like tattoos but he had one of his own within the week. His was a thermometer.

"Why a thermometer?" Serita asked.

"I dunno. So I can show how hot I am for you?!" Even he thought the comment was lame.

Other tattoos soon followed. Serita got one of an elephant standing on its hind legs. She loved the circus, but Ringling Bros. and Barnum & Bailey had been bullied into discontinuing the elephant act by PETA and then closed down, and she missed them.

Dirk spent a whole Saturday morning getting the Seven Dwarfs across his back. He had always loved that movie. Unfortunately, the tattoo artist misspelled "Dopey." But Dirk liked it. "It sort of fits, don't you think?" he said when he showed it to Serita.

It wasn't too long before their arms and upper bodies were filled with tattoos. Serita generally stuck with flowers of some kind, except for the one of the Lord's face on one of her butt cheeks – "because the Lord is so handsome."

That made Dirk more daring, and he got one of the Apostles on *his* butt cheek. "It looks more like Mary Magdalene, don't you think?" he said when he showed it to Serita. She agreed.

Soon their legs had tattoos as well. Dirk got one of a baby's cherubic face. Serita got two cherubs with wings coming out of their necks. After a while, they both got three angel baby faces on their kneecaps. When they knelt to pray, which they did often, the angel babies smiled.

Alas, their story did not end well. They eventually had so many tattoos, and no babies of their own, they both got septic poisoning. Dirk passed on, while Serita was pregnant from their Last Time Together. The baby was born seven months after Dirk died, and it had a birthmark in the form of Satan's face on top of the baby's actual face.

You should not make *graven images*, even of your wonderful would-be babies, or you will displease God, because He is a jealous God.

III. THOU SHALT NOT TAKE THE NAME OF THE LORD IN VAIN

THE FATHER, a sperm donor to a lesbian via a midwife, liked his resulting son very much. In fact, he was paying for the boy's trip to London: a theatre course, a hotel room, a gym membership, meals, you name it. Zoltan was twenty-two, tall, worked out, and was macho and reserved in speech. He was heterosexual, but what can you do?! Except love them, thought his gay father.

His father, Troy, was about to retire from his college teaching job back in the States ("not soon enough") and was a little portly, a little handsome, and in a non-committed relationship with Gary, who didn't like to travel. Gary liked to look after their six cats. He was trying to find a tall ramp so the cats could go out to pee in the backyard by climbing down from the fire escape at the condo. It was all part of that "gay lifestyle." (Forbidden by the Old Testament: Thou Shalt Not Have Six Cats.)

Troy took his son on the second day to see the British Museum, which had not lost its charm and was free besides. They both liked the Egyptian mummies and the Elgin Marbles, but museums get tiring and they didn't stay long.

The next day, Zoltan, at a pub, introduced himself to a group of Americans his age and said, "If I tell you a joke, can I join you?" His father saw it happen.

They said yes, and he did join them. His father, who made his living talking, was impressed. I'd never have the nerve to do that, he thought.

Naturally, one of the girls in the group "liked" Zoltan and they made a date – *voila!* – to go to the British Museum the following day. "It's a cheap date," Zoltan said. "Don't get married!" his father wisecracked. But Zoltan decided he didn't like the girl after all.

"You could see little hairs on her face, from the light pouring into the museum," he said.

So his son was still on the prowl "for girls" to "go out with" while he was in London.

The ladies in the theatre class all loved Zoltan and made a fuss over him, but they were all over sixty. "Some of them scare me," Zoltan said.

The "hotel" they were staying in (separate rooms) wasn't really a hotel but a student dormitory, fourteen storeys high with an inner courtyard containing old benches and a brick walkway. A mangy red fox had been spotted running between some bushes there. "Shall we go hunting for it?" Zoltan said. "Don't you dare," his father said. Troy was against guns and things like that. "That's why God invented the gun," Zoltan wisecracked. They both loved animals and were atheists, actually.

Troy caught a cold and it got worse, so he went to a medical clinic nearby. The London streets were still a bit tricky even after all Troy's visits, so he had a hard time finding it. He had to wait four hours. He also seemed to be getting a sty in his left eye. He took the business card from the medical clinic. You never know, especially when traveling abroad.

That night, Troy felt too ill to go out to the theatre or dinner. So Zoltan said that he wouldn't go, either. "There's a TV in one of the rooms downstairs," the father told the son. "Yeah, but it's British TV," the son said. Whatever that meant.

Later Troy was looking out his window at the courtyard and could see a bunch of young people in the tower across the way. They were laughing and whooping it up. He thought he caught a glimpse of Zoltan with a bottle of beer in one hand. It could have been somebody else.

A few minutes later, there was a knock at Troy's dorm door.

Zoltan held up his finger. Literally. He held up his little finger with his other hand.

"My God, what happened?" his father said.

"I was fooling around with some girls, sitting on the hallway floor with my arm behind me, and I kicked this big, heavy fire extinguisher off the wall by accident. It somehow fell on my finger." He indicated the severed pinkie of his left hand.

Troy felt lousy from the bad cold and the sty, but his parental side took over. "Didn't anybody over there help you?"

"Naw, didn't need it," his son said, very macho.

"We've got to get you to a hospital," Troy said.

"Goddamn it!" Zoltan swore. He looked like he was going to explode. But he kept his voice low.

"Maybe we can go to that medical clinic I went to. It's on Gower Street."

"I managed to pick up my finger," Zoltan said. "Goddamn me for not seeing that fire extinguisher."

"They can re-attach it if we get there in time!"

They decided to walk to the medical clinic. It wasn't that far away. There would be a doctor there, if it was still open. Zoltan had wrapped the severed finger in a napkins that Troy had in his room. But they couldn't find the medical clinic.

Troy was frantic. What was that address again?

"Oh, it doesn't matter," Zoltan said.

"It's your finger, for God's sake!"

"It's just my pinkie."

"You can't lose that!"

They searched for the address. Their cell phones weren't charged. A private doctor's office they passed didn't answer.

"Let's take a taxi to a hospital!" Troy kept saying. "They'll be open for sure."

"Goddamn it," Zoltan said, never raising his voice. "It doesn't matter. It's not bleeding anymore."

"Let's get a taxi! A taxi!" Troy couldn't see a taxi to save his life. In a city of taxis.

Neither one would scream for help. It wasn't manly.

Under his breath, Zoltan said "Goddamn, Goddamn" many times, but he lost the pinkie. He kept it in a jar back home and later told his kids, "That's the day I became a man." He never learned to play the piano, not that he would have.

That's what you get for taking the name of the Lord in vain, especially when it really is in vain, and instead of getting *actual treatment* for a severed finger because you're terrified of not "being a man," for God's sake!

IV. KEEP HOLY THE SABBATH DAY

WHY GOD HAD rested on the Seventh Day had always troubled Joshua Kleinborg, even though he had been raised by non-believing Jewish parents. If He was God, why did He need to rest? This doubt nagged at Joshua's brain. So he read up on the Sabbath and learned that Shabbat was the same thing, with prohibitions against doing laundry, turning on lights, writing, even erasing, and other things. He wondered if he had sinned because he had once erased a note he had written to his mother telling her off. He wondered if he had actually committed two sins: not honoring his mother by writing the note in the first place and then erasing it on a Sunday. He remembered that it was a Sunday because Joshua remembered things like that. He was very smart and studious. He was also "so handsome" and well-groomed and "brimming with information" – or was that just his grandmother bragging on him?

He read further and discovered that Keeping Holy the Sabbath had been a large part of Puritan thinking too. They were as militant about not working on the Sabbath as they were about working hard the other six days of the week. They even forbade gambling and shopping, and you had to listen to sermons. Joshua read some of the old sermons and thought they were "cute." He likewise went to some black churches in his city and listened to the sermons there. They were full of fire and brimstone about the Sabbath and how it should be honored. The preachers, he noticed, also spent a great deal of their sermons saying that the "practicing homosexuals" were going to burn in Hell for their depravity. Joshua did not find these latter-day sermons as "cute" as the old ones. You see, Joshua was one of these "homosexuals," although he hadn't actually "practiced" yet. "I have time," he told himself. "I am only thirty."

Joshua decided that, instead of becoming a "practicing homosexual," he would try to Keep Holy the Sabbath. He sat in his bathtub every Sunday morning and read more seventeenth-century Protestant sermons in a big book he found in a bookstore. In the afternoon, he always took a nap. In the evening, he would sit alone in his easy chair, and, out of principle, not watch TV but stare at the walls. Despite his best efforts not to, sometimes he would imagine that he saw figures of men on the walls doing things to each other. But he couldn't be sure and tried to think of all the Commandments.

Keep Holy the Sabbath was his favorite, by far, but he also enjoyed the other nine.

One evening – a Sunday, no less – Joshua went out to a gay club that he had heard about. He had grown weary of sermons and prohibitions and the walls of his apartment. He was thinking about going home with the middle-aged gentleman with the cowlick who had approached him and chatted him up. "What are you into?" the gentleman had asked.

Before he could come up with an answer, which would have been "kissing and hugging followed by rubbing and shooting," there was a commotion in the club and the patrons all started screaming and running every which way. A lone gunman had entered the club and begun blasting his AR-15 at the "homosexuals" he knew to be there.

Yes, Joshua was one of the casualties, shot two times in the head by the lone gunman. No, it's not funny, and perhaps if Joshua had violated the Sabbath more, and sooner, plus several other stupid Commandments, he would at least have had a few pleasant orgasms before he died.

V. HONOR THY FATHER AND THY MOTHER

"ARE YOU STILL SUCKIN' COCK?" his father wanted to know. It was the Fourth of July and eighty-nine degrees in Cleveland. They were sitting under the metal awning in the backyard of his parents during Rory's annual visit. They kept their interactions down to once a year now, but it was still a chore. His father sat there with the big glass of iced tea (laced with sugar) in his hand, his checkered shirt sweaty, some armpit hair showing through a rip in one arm. That rip had been there for years, but his father refused to have it fixed or get a new shirt. Whenever Rory would point it out, his father would say, "I bet you seen a lot worse than armpit hair in your time." Then he'd salute his son with the iced tea.

Rory had long since learned not to try banter with his father over his sexuality. He had expected the man to be resistant, then grow into acceptance, and eventually embrace his gay son just like he did their straight son, Mack. Only it hadn't worked out that way. His father had never accepted it and, if anything, seemed to be getting worse about the topic, even cruder, as if Rory's coming out had liberated him to say exactly what he was thinking, and in the crudest language he could think of. At least it was just once a year now, for three days, and then Rory could go back to San Francisco.

Rory was forty-five and in good shape. He worked out at the 23-Hour Fitness Center near his apartment and ate almost vegetarian: no red meat, very little dairy, fresh and unmanicured vegetables from a local produce shop. He kept his weight down and could live with the thinning hair. He was between partners, the last one having developed an obsession with drag and then moved to a Kollective in the woods in Oregon known as the Floral Pansy Boys. Todd and Rory had talked it over, but it wasn't really Rory's thing. He was hopeful that he would meet somebody new and nice somewhere.

"How's that Carmen Miranda boyfriend of yours?" his father was asking. Rory had made the mistake of bringing Todd to his folks' place in Cleveland one year.

"We're no longer together," Rory said, letting it go at that.

"You gays can't seem to make your relationships work, can you? How many guys does that make for you now?"

"Sometimes it's better to move on," Rory said. He almost said, "Like you and mom should."

His mother was coming out of the back door of the house, negotiating the rail-less, wobbly stairs that led down to the backyard. She had grown very stout in the last ten years and had started wearing a girdle again after many years – to keep "my girlish figure," but it wasn't working. She'd also begun wearing her faded brown hair extremely short. She looked like some of the old dykes Rory would see in San Francisco. He didn't think his mother had become a dyke, just more like the Midwestern grandma she was. She also had not accepted her son's coming out and liked to quote the Eternal Word of God on the subject and for some reason was particularly fond of the phrase "son of Sodom."

Rory tried to forgive and love them both. After all, they had fed him and nurtured him and given him baseballs, footballs, basketballs, and even horseshoes from the cradle. He wasn't a bad tennis player, but for his folks, who never watched tennis, that didn't count.

"So how are you two boys getting along?" his mother asked as she plopped down in the folding sun chair. Already some beads of sweat had trickled onto her forehead. She seemed to have a slight mustache now.

"Our boy's telling me about how to do analingus," his father said, exploding into a laugh.

"What's that?" his mother asked.

216

"Licking assholes!" Such merriment was hard to find in Cleveland.

Rory was not about to take the bait, no snotty reply to his dad, no patient explanation about what he did or did not do in bed.

"Oh, that's disgusting!" his mother said. "That's not good for you, Rory. Don't you know that?"

"How's Mack doing?" Rory said, changing the subject. There was nothing his mother liked talking about more than his brother.

"Amber Sue is going to have another baby!"

"Well, good for her! How many does that make now?"

"Six!" his father said. He smiled and took a long sip of his iced tea.

"Six?! That must more than satisfy your thirst for grandchildren," Rory said, hiding the edge on his words.

"They're scrumptious," his mother said. "I could just eat them up. And boisterous!" She looked as proud of her progeny as a peahen.

"I don't think I'd be good with kids," Rory said.

"Sure you would be," his mother said.

"I don't really like kids all that much."

"It doesn't matter when they're yours," his father said. "You like them then."

"Well, I love to see 'em come – and I love to see 'em *go*!" His mother laughed and patted at her damp forehead and mustache.

"Mack had a bad spell there," his father said. "That depression shit."

"Oh, I'm sorry to hear that," Rory said. He and his brother never spoke. They had barely spoken when they were kids.

"I told him to get off his fat ass and act like a man. His kids need him."

"And that boy pulled himself together and got a second job. And now they're all just fine," Rory's mother said. "When are you gonna find a wife and settle down, hon?" His mother just would never give up.

"You never know," Rory said to appease her.

"What's this I hear about you gays eatin' fecal matter?" his father suddenly said. "You'll have to give that up when you marry a girl."

"What are you talking about?" Rory knew better, but he couldn't resist.

"Yeah, I read about it on one of those Evangelical websites. Forty-six percent of the gays eat shit in their sexual practices."

"Are you sure it isn't more?" Rory said.

"Some percentage like that. That's why our ministers are going to Africa to spread the word about the gay lifestyle."

"Dad, are you sure you weren't reading about the amount of fecal matter that spatters on toothbrushes in the typical bathroom?" Rory shaded his eyes with his hand and wished he hadn't forgotten his sunglasses at home.

"I just don't get it, that's all. A man's supposed to fuck a pussy, and that's all! None of this slobberin' around down there." He toasted his wife. "Sorry, Mamma, for the language." His mother didn't respond this time. Most of the time she simply said with a wave of her hand, "Oh, him!"

And so the visit went, the same old, same old.

As Rory was packing to leave for home, he heard a commotion near the staircase in the living room that led up to the bedrooms. When he went in to see what it was, he found his father lying at the base of the staircase, out cold. His mother was kneeling beside him, crying as she felt his face.

"Did Dad fall down the stairs?" Rory asked his mother.

"I don't know. I don't know. It could have been a heart attack. His doctor told him his heart was bad."

Rory knelt next to his father. His mother went over to the Life Station button she kept on a string on a doorknob and pushed a button. After six rings, a male voice came on: "This is Life Station. Are you all right, Mr. and Mrs. Pearsall?"

"It's my husband! It's my husband!" Rory's mother kept saying, hysterical.

Then suddenly the power in the house went off, as did the voice of Life Station.

"What happened?" Rory asked his mother.

"Oh, we've had some bad fuses in the basement," she explained. "I told him and told him to get them fixed!"

By the time they re-established contact with Life Station and the ambulance came, Rory's father was dead. Rory had had to use his smartsphone and that had taken some time.

And Rory had not hurried.

VI. THOU SHALT NOT KILL

LILA WAS A STRONG WOMAN, it goes without saying these days, at seventy still a beauty, with gray-golden hair, lots of red lipstick, lots of cleavage, lots of earrings, a Ph.D. in Educational Empowerment from NYU. Lila was also Jewish, Reform. She had two male children, both doctors, from her two-year-long marriage many years ago to a man who was a doctor but who smoked too much marijuana and fooled around on the side with his patients. Lila had dropped him at age thirty but still took alimony from him once a month even though her doctor sons were rich and long gone off on their own. "He was a bastard, that husband!" Lila would justify herself.

When she retired at sixty-eight, she was not ready to leave her teaching job at a community college. She loved her students, and they loved her; still, she was, by her own admission, getting a bit forgetful: curriculum committee meetings, which classroom she was supposed to be in at one P.M., even the combination to the lock on her office door. So Lila retired.

She had a nice apartment in Queens, but like many before her, she found herself, retired, to be lonely. And horny. She flew all the way across the States to have sex with a gentleman she had met on a Seniors Discovery Trip to Ecuador. He lived in Utah. He had bragged that he had ten inches and Lila was a bit intrigued. But when she got to his house, he was too big and didn't fit. He also shot his load as he was trying to get inside and couldn't get another hard-on the rest of that weekend. She went on many websites and looked at photographs of potential suitors, lovers, or husbands. They were ordinary men, no doubt lying about their real ages, just as Lila lied about hers ("a sprightly 55"), but she found none of the men attractive. "What can you tell from a picture?!" Lila complained. She did manage to go on a few "dates." The dates were either too big or too small. "I feel like Goldilocks!" Lila said. "Where is Mr. Right Size?"

Then one day, Lila got a telephone call from a man with what she thought to be a Jamaican accent. She was going to hang up because it was an unsolicited call, but the Jamaican was lilting and charming and Lila was bored. He finally got around to the reason for the call. He had seen her picture on a dating website and found her "so lovely" that he just had to seek her out. They agreed to meet in a public place, a cafe a block from her apartment. He would be sporting a goatee and wearing a blue sweater, white pants, and a tam. Lila got ready by buying a low-cut dress, fancy high heel shoes, and a yellow scarf that flattered her green eyes.

Unfortunately, Tremaine did not show up at the cafe, so Lila had an espresso by herself and read the Sports section of *The New York Times*, all that was available in the cafe. When she got back to her apartment, there was a message blinking on her voice mail. It was from Tremaine. He apologized profusely that he had been unable to make their appointment. He said "so lovely" at least eight times in his one-minute message. Lila wrote him off.

But two days later, Tremaine called, and she was home. He was effusive with apologies and begged her to meet with him. She said no, she said no, she said no, and then she said yes. She put on the new dress, the high heels, and the scarf again and went to the same cafe. There were several Jamaicans there – she asked several black men – but not *her* Jamaican. "All right, enough of this crap!" Lila vowed. But Tremaine called again, and this time they talked for an hour: about growing up biracial in Jamaica, having three homes, one in Jamaica, one in Manhattan, and the third in Aspen, the difficulty of being endowed with eleven inches, and, of course, for Lila the ingratitude of her two doctor sons, who never called and didn't want her to visit because she was too messy. By the end of the phone conversation, Lila had agreed to send Tremaine a check for nine thousand dollars, which he had generously offered to invest for her in the same company that had doubled his money. They made plans to meet at the cafe. He would give her a receipt for the nine thousand dollars check then.

Lila was about to write the check when she got a call from Tremaine. "It's best you send the nine thousand dollars to me by MoneyGram," he explained. "It's safer. Checks can be stolen." Lila agreed.

Just before he hung up, Tremaine had a sudden idea. He had heard from his "financial adviser" in Jamaica who had just gotten approval of a special deal on mutual funds, and wondered if Lila might want to take advantage of the latest interest rate. So she tore up the check for nine thousand dollars and wrote one for sixteen thousand dollars. She had to dip into her pension balance to have enough. When she expressed some hesitation, Tremaine said, "You double your money in one swell foop." She laughed at his misuse of English and went off to a shop to send the MoneyGram to the address he had given her.

The next day, she got a phone call from "a friend of Tremaine's," also Jamaican, who said that Tremaine was sick and in bed and that he couldn't pick up the payment from MoneyGram because it was addressed to Tremaine. "You must help Tremaine and send new payment," Tremaine's friend implored. Lila was suspicious, but she was into it now. She sent another payment of sixteen thousand dollars, again taken from her pension fund. The clerk at the MoneyGram station said, "Didn't you already send this?"

"Mind your own business," Lila said. "I know what I'm doing." "Sorry," the clerk said. Both payments cleared that same day, and Lila waited for another call from Tremaine thanking her. Who knew – he might even have a fat check ready to give her!

After three days, Lila began to grow anxious. She had heard nothing from Tremaine or even Tremaine's friend. Oh, God, what have I done? she thought.

Then Tremaine did call, full of apologies and saying he had been "near death," but now was "much better, thank you" and he wanted to buy her an "expensive lunch" at the cafe.

Lila put on the new dress, the new shoes, and wrapped the new scarf around her neck to hide the veins on the sides that somehow looked more prominent than they had.

She waited in the cafe for an hour and a half. Tremaine did not show up.

The story might have ended there, but Lila was not about to be abused and cheated. She took a week to recover. She took back the dress and the scarf and got a refund. She contacted a lawyer and asked how she could get back her $32,000. "Do you have the man's full name or a real address?" the lawyer queried. "No," Lila admitted. "Then there is not much you can do, I'm afraid."

Lila's heart hardened at that moment. A huge, dark, and vicious cloud fell upon her soul. She went into the back bedroom that she never used and searched through some old boxes in the back of the closet. Eventually, she found the Glock .22 pistol that she had bought years earlier when she thought her ex-husband was going to cut off the alimony and that he might even arrange a contract killing of her. "There's no telling what that prick would do!" she'd said at the time. The Glock .22 was tucked in a blanket and still fully loaded. She wondered if the bullets would still be good. Did bullets get old? She put the gun in her purse.

She tried to find the phone numbers of Tremaine and Tremaine's friend, and she did. But they were "out of service." She waited. Something told her that one or both of them would call again. Sure enough, Tremaine's friend called two days later. "Do you want your $32,000 back?" he asked her.

At first she was surprised, but then, of course, he said that he would need another ten thousand dollars in a MoneyGram in order to get the $32,000 out of a bank in Kingston and "other stuff."

"You wind up with sixty-five thousand dollars!" he announced proudly.

"You sound very clever," Lila told him. "But I want a receipt for my money."

"You don't trust me?"

"Oh, I trust both you and Tremaine."

"Sorry we didn't call. Very busy."

"So why don't you bring by the receipt today? I'll give you cash."

"That's all you want, just a receipt?"

"I know I can trust you two to give me a valid one."

"I don't know."

"I can leave the door to my apartment ajar."

"What?"

"I think it's sexy, don't you? I'll buzz you in. There's an outside door and also my apartment door. Do you think you can find your way to me? I'll be waiting with the cash in bed."

"You'll be waiting in bed for me?"

"I like hot sex," Lila said. It was a plot she had lifted from "Forensic Files," the TV crime show, but it was the best she could come up with. "Have you got ten inches?"

"No, seven. Do you still want me to come?"

"Close enough. Let's say three P.M."

At two-thirty, Lila put on a negligee and robe, put the Glock .22 into her bed, under the pillow, opened her apartment door a crack, and waited there by the buzzer.

Promptly at three, Tremaine's friend rang her doorbell, identified himself, and Lila let him in. She ran back into her bedroom and got into the bed.

A few minutes later, Tremaine's friend said, "Mrs.?" cautiously, outside Lila's bedroom door.

"Close the apartment door," she called.

He went back and did so.

She briefly flirted with the idea of shooting him after the sex instead of before. But then she stuck with her original plan.

He slowly pushed open the bedroom door. "You sure about this?" he asked. He was short and ugly.

"Show me the receipt and show me your seven inches," she demanded, though she was shaking.

He showed her both. "Where's the cash?"

She let him get halfway across the shag carpeting before she took the Glock .22 and shot him through the forehead. The police didn't doubt Lila for a minute when she told them about the intruder who had intended to rape her and the apartment door she had forgotten to lock. They even had the body, with its open fly, removed and the blood spots on the carpeting cleaned, once they had taken all the photos they wanted. Lila did not show them the receipt, which was not worth the paper it was written on.

It took her over a year to hear from Tremaine again. He said that he hadn't heard from his friend and wondered what had happened to him. She didn't think the police would believe her if she shot a second Jamaican rapist in her bedroom. So this time, she invited him to come at twilight to a vacant lot she'd seen on a street on the other side of Queens. She told him that she'd have cash for him and "maybe a little kiss." Naturally, one thing led to another in the vacant lot and she shot him through the side of the neck just as he was thrusting into her and telling her she was "a stupid bitch, my bitch."

She didn't get her money back, her pension never quite recovered, and she never found a man to her liking; nevertheless, Lila for the rest of her life felt a satisfaction that transcended mere sex.

VII. THOU SHALT NOT COMMIT ADULTERY

ARLENE FAXON had always been a "good girl," even when she was nearing forty. Her Roman Catholic upbringing had been thorough. The indoctrinating virgin nuns of the Order of the Immaculate Heart of Mary had schooled her well in various prohibitions, especially those involving "purity." She also did not have a very strong sex drive, and so she left unexplored "that side" of life and concentrated on her studies and got her A.A. degree. She was a tall, angular girl with rather small eyes in a rather pudgy face who'd had only two dates in high school, both with a boy that she later found out to be "mental." She supposed that she would be married one day to "a nice man" who "loved" her. Where this man would come from was vague. Arlene did not make any attempts to find him. She knew that she lived in the Technological Age, and she had Twitter, Facebook, and Snapchat accounts, yet she almost never used them. She worked as a Notary Public in a walk-in law office in Daly City, California. She visited her elderly parents every Sunday and went to a movie once a month, always a comedy. She could easily have been living in 1952.

Then one day, a client who had used her Notary Public skills several times asked her out to lunch. His name was George Liddy and he said he was a lawyer "between jobs." He looked to be about forty, like her, a bit hunchy in the shoulders, but not too bad, balding on top, but with manicured fingernails and a dry wit. He had a smile that, as they say, was winning.

At lunch, George spelled out in great detail his lawsuit with the makers of Cialis, the male "enhancement" drug. Apparently, he'd gotten melanoma on the back of his neck from using the drug. Fortunately, it did not show when he let his hair in the back grow long. There was a new scar from his first treatment. He offered to show her, but Arlene declined. He asked her if she ever felt "romantic."

She pretended she didn't hear him as the waitress wanted to know if they wanted any pie.

She told her parents about the "date" that she had been on with George.

"Is he the one?" her mother asked, hopefully.

"You're almost forty!" her father reminded her.

"I'm already forty," Arlene replied.

"I want some grandbabies!" her father said. He was getting deaf and talked too loudly.

Arlene kissed them goodbye and took home some of her mother's German Chocolate Decadence Cake.

She did not pursue George. She thought he was probably married and just looking for a "little bit on the side." Arlene did not see herself as a little bit on the side.

But then George was "in the neighborhood" and asked her to lunch again. She offered to pay for the two of them, but he said "no way." She sort of liked that. At one point, she asked, "Are you married?"

He hesitated, smiled, and then said, "I was. I've been divorced for two years."

"Any children?" she wondered.

"No. God didn't see His way to blessing us with children," George said.

They chatted and nibbled and had a good time. As he walked Arlene back to her office, he seemed moody. "Is something wrong?" she asked him.

"Not really," he said. "I'm just wondering about us."

"Us?" Arlene's breath was taken away. "What do you mean – us?"

"I like you, Arlene. I'd like to see more of you."

She was flattered but reluctant.

"You don't like me?"

She didn't know if she liked him or not. It was only two lunches. And she'd never ask somebody if they liked *her*.

"Maybe we could catch a movie together," she said. "I prefer comedies."

"Comedies are sort of silly, aren't they?" George said.

"I like them."

"Okay, a comedy it will be."

The next Monday, they went to a silly comedy starring a black comedian who screamed a lot.

George asked Arlene if she wanted to come back to his place.

"Isn't it rather soon for that?" she said.

He laughed. "Life is short."

She did not go back to his place, and she did not invite him to hers. She let him kiss her on the mouth when they said goodnight. Arlene was pretty sure that she would never see George again. And she was already regretting the goodnight kiss.

She spent a good part of the next month fretting over George, who did not stop by for lunch or call her. She wondered if she had let her one chance for marriage get away. Oh, George Liddy most likely wanted just one thing! she told herself. And he was not getting that until they were married. The Sisters of the Immaculate Heart of Mary would be proud of her! People waited for "that" until they were married. There were certain principles that people, good people, did not violate.

Then, out of the blue, she found George's business card in a stack on her desk and called him.

He seemed very happy to hear from her. "I'm sorry I haven't been in touch, Arlene. I got wrapped up in that Cialis lawsuit."

"How's that going?" she asked.

"Too soon to tell. It's very cutting edge."

To cut to the chase, Arlene went out to dinner that evening with George and they went back to his place. She broke the Fifth or Sixth Commandment, depending on how you count, concerning adultery, and violated the prohibition that the good nuns had so carefully instructed Arlene about. She even realized that George was probably still married. He seemed to forget how much he had told her and mentioned that the divorce was "almost final."

She remained a virgin technically even after that long night. It turned out that George's idea of sex was that he stick his long, skinny penis down Arlene's throat until she gagged. He liked to do it over and over, and that's the *only* thing he liked to do. "You like to eat that goddamned dick, don't you?!" he asked repeatedly.

No, she didn't. So Arlene did not marry George Liddy. In fact, she never saw him again, and she was always grateful that she had broken the Fifth or Sixth Commandment, unlike so many millions before and after her who regretted *not* having premarital sex and only finding out too late, after marriage, what horrors were in store for them sexually.

VIII. THOU SHALT NOT STEAL

AT THE FUNERAL of Elbert Malachi Macintosh his unmarried son and his married daughter had just publicly viewed the body, which looked old and stiff and surprisingly brown-faced. It was because of the makeup the funeral director had applied. This was the same funeral director who had cruised the son at the earlier viewing before the public was allowed in: "I hear you aren't married out there in California. I'm not married here in Farmersville." The son, Guy, had let the overture pass. Guy was forty-one and beginning to lose his looks, so the overture was nice, only his father's funeral was not the time or the place. He had said, "Can you make my father's face less brown?" But the funeral director hadn't done so.

His half-sister, Marge, from Guy's father's first marriage, was fifty-five and had every malady known to womankind: obesity, bowel blockage, nearly blinding cataracts, rotted food that got lodged behind her heart, and dehydration that required her to carry around a thermos of drinking water at all times. Aside from these issues, Marge was very jolly and always praised God for her health. "Nobody likes a complainer," she always said.

Guy and Marge, although related by blood, had not really spent much time together. She had run off to have an "illegitimate" baby at fifteen (all very hush-hush at the time), when Guy was just a baby himself. She had supposedly left the infant with an aunt and then run off and had another "illegitimate" baby with the same man, who wouldn't marry her. Guy, when he had learned of the two "illegitimate" children, both of whom had died after a few months, did not approve. Although gay, he was something of a prude and thought that people who had babies should take proper care of them. So he and Marge barely knew each other. He also lived in San Francisco and she in Springfield, Illinois.

So their paths did not cross that much.

They had clashed a bit during the funeral arrangements. Marge wanted an expensive coffin, Guy wanted a moderately priced one. "Nobody's going to see the casket when it's in the grave. We're talking about the time it's in the church, and even then it will be mostly covered up!" he argued.

Marge didn't see it that way. "You have only one father," she said. "You don't act like a cheapskate with your own father."

"Our own father was a cheapskate, you know that. He wouldn't want us to waste money on an expensive casket."

"Well, I'm sorry you didn't love our father enough to . . ."

Guy realized that Marge had done the heavy lifting of looking after their father in those final years, every week driving the twenty-one miles from Springfield to Farmersville and taking care of "things" as best she could with her many ailments, even getting their father to talk that last year, when he had been so close-mouthed, so reticent, his whole life, beyond the point of neurosis. "I don't think he'd want the expensive casket!" Guy insisted.

"What about cremation?" Marge asked. "I think he'd want to be cremated."

"I doubt that," Guy said. "He hated the idea of being burned up. I remember him distinctly saying, one of the few times he said anything, that being cremated was like going to Hell while you're still on Earth."

"That's funny. The last time Homer and I came down here to look after him, Dad distinctly said 'I prefer to be cremated.'"

"Dad never used the word 'prefer' in his life!"

"Well, I was here, and where were you?"

"I guess I was back in San Francisco working eighty hours a week to earn money for the casket you apparently think we must have!"

"I'll pay for the casket!" Marge snapped. "You don't need to worry."

"Well, you forgot to pay dad's ambulance bill last year!" Guy snapped right back. "I don't want a bill for the casket coming to my house!"

"Homer and I were havin' a little trouble with our bills at that time."

"I didn't mind paying the bill," Guy said. "But I wish you had kept up their Medicare. We wouldn't have had to pay at all."

"Oh, that Obamacare was too hard to keep track of!" Marge kept right on snapping.

"What about this funeral home – how much is that going to cost?" Guy asked.

"I'm not sure. This is a small town. It shouldn't be that bad."

"Famous last words," Guy said.

"Have you seen the graves?" Marge wanted to know.

"I have not."

"Homer and I can drive you out there, on the edge of town, if you want."

"I don't want to see their graves."

"Why not?"

"The thought of their bodies lying out in the middle of nowhere with snow on top of their skeletons is too much. My mother's there too."

"It's a pretty cemetery."

"No cemetery is pretty," Guy said.

They left the details of their father's funeral unfinished and walked out of the Viewing Room and into the vestibule. They both noticed that there were several cardboard boxes with the label HOLY LATIN MASSES on them. The boxes held donations for Masses to be said by the parish priest for the soul of the named deceased party. One of the boxes had **"Elbert Malachi Macintosh"** handwritten on it.

"It's donations to Dad for Latin Masses," Guy said.

"How many are there?"

They both looked into the box. There seemed to be about a hundred.

Marge opened one and saw a ten-dollar bill along with the Mass card. Guy opened one and found two twenty-dollar bills.

"What do you think?" Marge said. She had never been all that religious, what with the "illegitimate" babies and such. Guy had left the Church at twenty-one after he sucked his first dick.

"I don't think Dad needs a hundred Masses, even if they're in Latin," Marge said.

"I think you're right," Guy said. "He's already going to Heaven."

The two went through the Mass cards and removed them all and took out the cash and carried away the empty envelopes as they left. They agreed to spend the money on the cost of the funeral home and other expenses. They decided to come back and leave three Mass cards so that it wouldn't look too suspicious.

They still did not see one another very often, but they had bonded over the money not wasted on Holy Latin Masses and became very good pen pals and even said some Masses (sort of, and in English) for their dead father for free.

IX. THOU SHALT NOT BEAR FALSE WITNESS AGAINST THY NEIGHBOR

ROXY RAN AN ESCORT SERVICE out of her rent-controlled apartment in San Francisco. She had tried making it into an Airbnb, but it wasn't in the best neighborhood, shall we say, and so Roxy didn't get many customers for mere overnight stays.

So Roxy decided to run the escort service instead. She was the only escort, although she didn't tell the would-be customers that. She found out what they liked and dressed up in red wigs, blonde wigs, black wigs, Princess Leia hair-buns, or whatever they wanted. Underneath, she was herself, a thirty-seven-year-old Greek-American with big boobs, big hips, big lips, and no gag reflex. She got plenty of business almost immediately, and the word of mouth – about her mouth – was excellent. Although her clientele was not all she might have desired, they were mostly well-behaved: Chinese businessmen, Arabs who weren't terrorists, pimply Caucasian teenagers, and the occasional gay man fed up with the bar scene in San Francisco. Her prices were reasonable and she didn't blackmail anybody.

She sent her elderly mother in Nyack a check once a month to help with the bills and told her that she did a lot of overtime at the Pro Beauty Shoppe in San Francisco. She hadn't worked at the Pro Beauty Shoppe for seven years.

Roxy didn't particularly like sucking cock, but she did it, faking the gusto and charging a surcharge for swallowing. She thought about getting married, but she supposed any husband would expect head from her, and she gave enough of that at work. One of her clients was so taken with her that he proposed twice. But both times, he was drunk and his crotch smelled bad. The client took the rejection in stride. He was a cripple and a hunchback, sort of like Alexander Pope, only without the poetry. Roxy didn't like to hurt people's feelings, so she told the proposer she would "think it over" and he never came back.

Roxy had to look out for venereal diseases and had a bidet installed in her bathroom. She thought it was a genius invention. She charged extra for those who wanted to watch her use the bidet.

"Guys are kinky!" she said philosophically. "Mostly, they just want some release."

Everything was going along swimmingly: Roxy was paying all her bills and putting some money into the stock market, and she had her house redecorated. Some of the neighbors didn't like the new color of paint: an iridescent green. Why should it be drab and ordinary?! Roxy thought.

Then one day, one of her customers said that he had read about her services online. This came as news to Roxy. "I don't advertise online," she said.

"Well, you're there," said the client. He was a feminine gentleman who liked to dress up as President Donald J. Trump.

Roxy resisted, but finally, she checked the website in question. It was some sort of Complaints Online setup. She never used the Internet, thought it was just a fad.

She began reading the complaints:

"Roxy's is run out of the womans home. I came twice for one price. Highly recommended!"

Well, that didn't sound like a complaint exactly.

Roxy read on:

"Unlike the previous poster, I was not satisfied with the service at Roxy's!!!! I never did come and I only got to stay twenty minutes over my hour!!!! A real Rip-Off!!!!!!!!"

Well, fuck him, thought Roxy.

But then it got worse:

"I went to Roxy's Place on Fell Street and she doesn't run a brothel, no way! It's just a cookie store, unlicensed, with no sex whatsoever of any kind. The cookies were fine, especially the ginger snaps. But if it's sex you're looking for, Roxy's is not the place."

What was going on here?

That day there were forty-two additional complaints about Roxy's services. They had different names on them, but Roxy suspected they were all from the same guy: Abner H. He really had it in for her for some reason:

"I scheduled some S&M bondage at four last week, and all I got was an oatmeal cookie."

"The place is clean, but there is no hanky-panky at Roxy's. Go if you want a cookie, not nookie."

On and on the complaints went. Roxy noticed that the phone had stopped ringing. Two clients canceled and wouldn't listen to Roxy's protests that these postings were outrageous lies. One said, "How dare you just give cookies now and nothing else!" and hung up.

And it didn't stop. Day after day, the villainous Abner H kept posting lies about the lack of sexual activities of any kind at Roxy's.

Sad to report, Roxy soon went out of business due to these complaints and she had to go back to working at the Pro Beauty Shoppe, and Abner H burned in Hell for all eternity for bearing false witness.

X. THOU SHALT NOT COVET

WHEN HE WAS nearly one, Joey wanted a G.I. Joe doll, because his sister, Allison, had a new Barbie.

When Allison was three, she wanted a pony. She got a Golden Retriever.

When she was five, she wanted a different baby brother. She had to keep the same one.

At the age of six, Joey wanted a Detroit Tigers baseball card of Al Kaline.

At seven, Allison wanted a coloring book of Debbie Reynolds.

Her brother, Joey, wanted a coloring book of Sal Mineo.

When they were eight and nine, Joey and Allison wanted turbo something or other.

At ten, Joey wanted to go to Disneyland. They all went.

At twelve, Allison wanted a Pretty Miss makeup kit.

At thirteen, Joey wanted a new sister. The old sister was "snotty."

When her fourteenth birthday rolled around, Allison wanted Bobby Clarke to ask her out on a date.

On his fourteenth birthday, Joey asked for genuine leather moccasins.

On her fifteenth birthday, Allison asked for the Pill. Her parents said no.

On her sixteenth birthday, Allison asked for an abortion, like her friend Mary Jane's. Her parents said yes.

On Joey's sixteenth birthday, he asked for rubbers. His parents said no.

On Joey's seventeenth birthday, he asked for a STD test. He got one. And a box of rubbers.

At eighteen, Allison begged for those last three credits so that she could graduate from high school. She didn't get them.

Joey, at nineteen, begged that the Navy would overlook that shop-lifting incident he'd had at thirteen. It did.

When she was twenty-one, Allison hoped that her new husband, Randy, would look at her like he did at Melanie, her best friend.

At twenty-two, Joey hoped he'd get used to having one leg. Some war or other.

When twenty-three came around, Allison hoped that she'd never see Randy again. She did, because he had visitation rights to Randy, Jr.

Joey, at age twenty-five, had mastered his prosthesis and ran in the Paralympics. He came in fifth.

Allison ran for him when she was twenty-seven and he had lost his second leg in a car crash.

She came in second.

At thirty, Joey wanted one of those electrified wheelchairs.

At thirty-two, Allison wanted her second husband, Sal, to stop using hydrocodone cough syrup, the way her friend Marcie's husband had done.

At thirty-four, Allison wanted Sal to go to Re-Hab. He went to Hawaii on his father's credit card instead.

Joey, when he turned thirty-five, wanted to die and took some pills. They had been manufactured in mainland China and didn't work.

Allison at forty married Kenneth, who had a job at Walmart.

Joey wanted to feel better, so he drank lots of whiskey.

At forty-one, Allison rediscovered the Church and went twice on Sunday.

Joey at forty-two was behind in his rent and asked his elderly parents for a loan. They took out a second mortgage.

At fifty, Allison had a nervous breakdown and asked her parents if she could come and live with them "for a while."

At fifty-one, Joey had a Veterans Administration one-bedroom apartment that allowed pets. He got a rescue rabbit from Animal Control.

Allison, on her fifty-third birthday, had an operation on her hip. She prayed that she'd be able to walk again. She was able to but needed a cane.

Joey at fifty-three won $250 when he bought a scratch-off lottery ticket.

Allison came to visit Joey on his fifty-fourth birthday at his apartment. She hadn't called and he wasn't home. She left a note.

Joey saw the note but misplaced it, and so he didn't call his sister. He wasn't into Social Media.

At sixty, Allison won $40 in the Super Lotto.

When he was sixty-two, Joey got early Social Security. He splurged on a trip to Tijuana. He didn't like Tijuana. He saw a donkey there and sort of liked it.

At sixty-five, Allison wanted Beverly Hills MD Dark Circle Corrector for under her eyes.

Joey, at sixty-four, wanted Depend Shields for Men.

At seventy, Allison met Jerry and they got married at the Teeniest Chapel in Las Vegas.

Joey, although his wheelchair made it difficult, came to the wedding and also won $139 in the slot machines.

Back home, Joey's rabbit had died while he was in Las Vegas. So he got another one. He called it Funny Bunny. He still wanted a donkey, but they weren't allowed.

Allison enjoyed 2.3 years with Jerry until he developed a hernia and got cranky and abusive.

Joey drank two bottles of Jim Beam on his seventy-second birthday and barely got drunk.

Allison was worried about her brother and flew out to see him. But he was dead when she arrived. She discovered his body on the floor, turning green, and called Management.

Joey was buried in the Veterans' cemetery out by the Chevron refinery. The grave had a view of a scenic hill.

Allison died at age seventy-nine planning her new marriage to Lou. For a man of eighty, Lou had a nice ass.

(If it weren't for *coveting*, there would be no hope – and no business – in this world.)

[Did the elderly writer keep his promise to write "sweet" stories for a whole book?]

[No. But here's one more.]

NO GREATER LOVE

AMONG OTHER THINGS, Paul had to pee. His bladder had been letting him down for some time now, and as he sat in his rental car he could tell that he was going to wet his underwear. Yes, he could get out of the car and pee next to it, but he was pretty sure he had seen a wolf on the horizon. Would human urine repel or attract wolves? He wasn't sure. Damn, he should have done more research on the "wilds" of Canada before setting off from Vancouver on this cockamamie trip. He realized part of it was age, the Big Six-Oh and all that went with it, the thickening of his midsection, the man boobs, the crippling leg spasms in the middle of the night, with no sympathy from Hope, who had her own age and health problems and could barely hide her contempt for his. "Oh, stop whining!" she was always saying, her mouth tight and angry. She was right: she whined enough for the two of them.

The car trip was supposed to somehow restore his energy, his optimism, his manhood. It had been a lousy year at the real estate office, and his usual easements (red wine, MMA blood sports, sex with Hope with his eyes shut) were no longer working. He glanced through the windshield to see if that really was a wolf. He couldn't tell – his eyesight was going, too, and he wouldn't go in for glasses. He remained in the driver's seat and peed on himself. He pulled on his crotch to lessen the feel of the wetness and sighed. He looked in the back seat at the small pistol he had brought on the trip for security, a Ruger LC9. He had passed the background check with flying colors. What color are flying colors? he wondered vaguely. My life is so bland I can even buy a pistol and nobody cares. He got the pistol and waved it at the real or imaginary wolf on the horizon. "Stay away from me, shithead!" Paul threatened.

His voice disturbed Cookie, his ten-year-old Pomeranian, who had been sleeping on the back seat. She looked up at Paul and blinked a couple of times. There were black eye "boogers" at the edges of her eyes and her teeth were a bit yellow and worn. She was still alert, but she was up to ten pounds now. He dug some kibble out of the pet food bag also on the back seat. "Want some, Boo Boo?" he asked. She didn't. She got down off the seat and lapped up some water from her water dish, then hopped back onto the seat. All of a sudden, Cookie's ears pricked up and she put her paws on the passenger-side rear window. She growled.

"What is it, pretty girl?" Paul asked.

He looked where she was looking but couldn't see anything except the "wilds" of Canada, miles and miles of vacant terrain with sparse, ugly weeds, rocks, and dirt. So much for Travel Section lies!

He checked the pistol again. He had never fired one in his life and didn't approve of guns and had signed at least three petitions against firearms. He opened the pistol and noticed that there was only one bullet loaded, from the time the gun salesman had demonstrated how to load it. He looked under the rental car paperwork on the back seat for the box of ammunition he had bought at the same time as the pistol. Only it wasn't there. He looked on the floor in the back, thinking maybe Cookie had knocked the box off the seat. Nothing.

"What happened to the bullets, girl?" he asked. Then he remembered putting the box on the shelf in the garage next to where he always parked – so that he wouldn't forget it! No doubt it was still sitting there.

He looked out all the windows. It was getting toward dusk. Cookie growled, but not at him. "We'd better get back to the motel," he said. Oh, God, he'd have to sneak her in again. The damned No Pets rule and such a shabby motel at that! "This was a terrible idea, coming up here!" he cursed. "Never again!"

He turned the key in the ignition. The car started and then died. He took a moment to gather his thoughts and catch his breath.

Maybe I actually put the bullets in the glove compartment, he thought. He opened it, and there were no bullets there, just some maps and somebody's stale peppermint gum still in its wrapper. Maybe the bullets are in the trunk, he thought. He hesitated, but then he got out of the car and checked the trunk. Just a spare tire. He slammed the trunk door shut with all his might. He shaded his eyes with one hand and surveyed the landscape. Was that a ravine in the near-distance? It was getting chilly and he adjusted his old, torn jacket against the chill. Was that something on the horizon, only closer? Cookie was barking full throttle now, her little brown-mouthed face at the side back window, a tiny terror. Could she smell the wolves?

Paul got back into the car. He tried to calm Cookie down. "It's all right, girl. It's all right!"

But he knew it was not all right. There were now two "somethings" on the horizon. And maybe a third? And they looked like dogs. Big dogs. Bad dogs.

He picked up his mobile phone and put in his pass code. He got a message: SERVICE NOT AVAILABLE IN THIS AREA. Why wasn't that information in the Travel Section?!

He tried the ignition again. Still nothing. "Don't panic," he told himself. "You can handle this. You didn't plan it well, but you can get out of it."

Cookie was trying to get out of the car, jumping up and down on the back seat. She wanted to go after the "somethings" and rip their throats out. "You're not going anywhere, girl," Paul said. "Calm down. Calm down."

Out of the corner of his eye, he noticed something at the back of the car. He raised himself up enough to see better. He couldn't see anything. Yet there was something there. Cookie knew it as well and had stopped barking and was trembling. Her bright eyes were wide.

When Paul looked up, he saw the wolf. It was sniffing at the bumper. It did not appear to realize that Paul was inside the car. It looked hungry, sort of mangy, its mouth open in a slow pant.

Then it saw Paul and backed off. "Get out of here!" Paul shouted, waving his arms.

The wolf backed off further, but then stopped and glared at him, its eyes full of calm hate. Another wolf came up beside the first one and surveyed Paul inside his rental car. What should he do?

Should he yell at them and maybe scare them off? Should he just sit there and maybe they would go away? He tried starting the car again. All he got was a sluggish grinding and no turn over. He locked the four car doors, again. He searched for the missing packet of bullets. "Go, girl!" he said to Cookie. "Find bullets!" She jumped up and down and yelped. But she didn't find the bullets. "You're no help," he told her. No, the bullets were safe at home, on that shelf.

Maybe if he shot one of the wolves with the one bullet he had, the other wolves would get the message and run away? What if he only wounded it and it went berserk? Maybe the other wolves would come to its rescue and go berserk as well? And what if he missed it and that left him with no protection at all? Why didn't he know more about wolves?! Why hadn't he watched more of those wildlife series that were always on TV? Why hadn't he loaded more bullets? Why hadn't he just stayed home with Hope, as unpleasant as she had become? Even she was better than being devoured by wolves "in the wilds." He unlocked the door on the driver's side and put one leg out. He made some sort of noise deep in his throat to scare off the pack. He hoped it wasn't the sound prey makes when it's cornered. He held up the LC9 and banged it on the top of the car – to hell with dents. The three wolves ran away. "And stay away!" Paul yelled after them.

But the wolves' running away had emboldened Cookie, who jumped onto the driver's seat and then leapt out of the car and started chasing the wolves. "Oh, for God's sake, come back here!" Paul shouted after her. She kept running and barking and never looked back.

He took a few steps away from the car, then stopped. He had left the car keys in the ignition. Damn rental! His own car made a beeping noise if you did that. He started back for the car keys and then heard the gentle click as the car locked itself, a safety measure. Now he couldn't get back inside the car. He couldn't use his cell phone, either, which was locked inside the rental car anyway. And he couldn't see or hear Cookie any longer.

Paul came back nearer to the car and leaned against it. He was out of breath, and he hadn't even been running. He was thirsty and had to pee again. And his underwear was still wet. "Cookie! Come here, baby! Cookie, come!"

It grew darker and still the dog had not returned. He couldn't bear the thought of what might have happened to her, ripped to pieces, eaten alive. He couldn't lose her. She was all he had. Hope wouldn't care, in fact would be happy if Cookie was dead. She'd never liked pets. He rested his forehead on his forearm, which he had placed on the top of the car near the driver's seat. He tried all the four doors again, with the same result.

An hour passed and the darkness deepened. Maybe if he could survive the night, somebody would spot him in the morning. Yes, there were stories like that in the newspapers all the time.

But then, out of nowhere, Cookie was back! She had some brambles in her tail and was panting, but she didn't seem to be harmed in any way. "Thank God, thank God!" Paul said, grabbing her up into his arms. She licked his face but seemed to want down so that she could get back into the car. "I'm sorry, girl," he said. "We're locked out." She jumped up on the car door anyway, her nails clicking against the metal. "We'll make it through the night, okay?"

Cookie and Paul nestled against the rental car as best they could. He put her inside his jacket and their bodies helped heat each other. Around dawn, the wolves returned, six of them now. Paul stood up and counted them. They were headed right toward him in a ragged line. He felt the chill of "the wilds" engulf his body. He knew he could never outrun them. He could see them coming toward him, slinking, their teeth bared. They would be upon him one by one, savaging his neck, ripping his face. He felt every slash, every bite. Oh, God, make it quick! he thought. There's too much suffering in this life already. "Please don't let me die in agony, too!" It was the first prayer Paul had uttered in forty years.

The wolves reached him quickly. They stood a few yards away, watching him, waiting. They seemed to know that he couldn't get away. But what was that metal thing in his hand? Could that hurt them? They waited patiently. They had learned patience over the centuries. Cookie whimpered as she huddled inside Paul's jacket. "It's all right, pretty girl," he whispered to her. "It's all right."

As the first wolf moved toward them, Paul looked down at Cookie and knew he could not let her die this way. He placed the LC9 against the top of her head, hesitated, then fired the one bullet he had. The noise startled the wolves, who moved back a bit as Paul took off his jacket and laid Cookie's body in it. "Good night, girl," he said as he rested his back against the rental car and stilled his breath and waited for the wolves.

ON CHRISTMAS EVE

I RAN INTO SANTA on his sleigh today. He looked busy and stressed. He said that he was packing toys for kids everywhere. Cynically, I asked him about those six-year-old kids in Connecticut who had just been shot to death in their classroom by a madman. "*They* won't be home when you visit!" I snapped. Santa thought for a moment, then said, "I'll stop by Heaven on my job tonight."

[The old writer, after reading through his new collection of stories, decided to burn the whole batch. He tossed them into the fireplace, every draft of them.]

[No, he didn't. These are not burned up. They are here. And isn't that SWEET?]